I0677041

BABIES WITHOUT TAILS

BABIES
WITHOUT TAILS

Stories by Walter Duranty

WILDSIDE PRESS

www.wildsidepress.com

COPYRIGHT 1937 BY WALTER DURANTY

All rights in this book are reserved, and it may not be reproduced in whole or in part without written permission from the holder of these rights. For information address the publishers.

Some of the stories in this volume have appeared in Collier's, Red Book Magazine and a volume of short stories published by Coward-McCann.

Contents

BABIES WITHOUT TAILS

The Brave Soldier
and the Wicked Sorcerer

AS THE OLD TALES TELL, a brave young soldier came back to his village from the wars. He had fought three years in the Red Army, and at Perikop, when Wrangel's Death Battalion of ex-officers was annihilated in the bloodiest battle of the Civil War, he had won the Order of the Red Flag, now flaunting bronze and scarlet on his breast.

With envy the village fingered his gold watch, which rang small tinkling chimes when you pressed a button, and the silver cigarette case with its baronial crest. Peter Pavlovich was no Communist, and loot to the soldier is loot, be it ever so strictly forbidden.

Best of all, there was Marfa Ivanovna, his childhood's sweetheart. Their parents were friends, and well-to-do as peasants go. Fifteen acres of good farm land were already allotted to Peter and Marfa, and five more by virtue of his medal. The house would be built in a few weeks, with a lean-to stable for the cow and the horse. The bride would bring a dowry of furniture and household gear.

Life smiled, it seemed, for the young couple, as they wandered in the melting snow of the village street happy as if the flowers of summer were already bright on the fields. But alas, in that Eden a serpent lurked. One morning Marfa was sad and downcast when Peter greeted her.

"What's wrong?" he cried.

She shook her head and would not speak.

At length, as they sat hand in hand beside the river, she told him in gasping phrases, with round, tearful eyes. The Khaldoon had summoned her the night before; the Khaldoon, that survival of the

1

The Brave Soldier and the Wicked Sorcerer

past in many a Russian village — wizard, sorcerer, master of spells and potions, suspect of commerce with the powers of darkness.

"There are evil spirits leagued against your marriage," he had declared. "I have heard voices and seen visions. In the Middle World, between earth and hell, you have enemies, who must be propitiated. A dark Fate hangs over you, and I alone can help. Even by chance should you defeat the Strange Ones, their vengeance would pursue you. Unless you accept my aid your baby will be hairy all over and have a long black tail."

Terror and maidenly embarrassment melted poor Marfa to tears upon her lover's breast. But they learn more than fighting in the Red Army, and Peter was made of stern stuff.

"What will it cost?" he asked shrewdly.

"Twenty rubles," she sobbed. Then in a lower tone, "But think, Peterkin, a baby with a long black tail!"

"Don't be silly," snapped the young man. "Twenty rubles for that old crook! He can't frighten me with his nonsense."

How can timid girlhood prevail against a warrior with medals won in battle? An hour later Peter and Marfa, in their Sunday finery, were jolting through the slush to the house of the priest at the other end of the village. They would get married right away, without telling anyone; on that he was determined. The wedding feast could come later. Once the Holy Church had sanctified their union, there was no risk, he had convinced her, of long-tailed babies.

But as the shaggy pony trotted down the hill into the hollow where the priest's house stood, a Portent came. From the icy slough beside the road there arose a monstrous pig, growling so horridly that the horse upreared in fright. The sleigh skidded, tipped on one runner, and threw them out into the mud.

As bridegrooms soon discover, a man can bend a woman to his will, but he cannot mold her thoughts. Marfa held out her skirt, all stained and wet.

2

The Brave Soldier and the Wicked Sorcerer

"Just look!" she wailed. "I knew this would happen. . . . My best dress. . . . It's begun, I tell you! It's begun!"

"What do you mean?" asked the boy, as he shouldered the sleigh back onto the road. "What's begun?"

"The demons!" she cried. "They've begun already . . . to spoil our marriage. . . . Or the Khaldoon himself."

Peter, of course, was a hero. But even the Red Army is unused to monstrous growling pigs. His hair prickled at the roots. Then fright gave way to fury.

"The Khaldoon, is it?" he shouted. "I'll show him what it means to interfere with me." And snatching the knife from his belt he sprang upon the pig and stabbed it in the neck.

The pig died hard, as pigs will, with loud shrill whistling screams. The girl looked proudly at her lover, and clung to his avenging arm. Peter clucked to the horse and swung it towards the little lane leading to the priest's house.

Suddenly he was halted by a bellow. Across the half-melted snow scurried the priest himself, a stout red-faced man with a bushy gray beard, his smock tucked up to his knees.

"My pig!" he shouted. "Who has hurt my pig? My fine fat Easter pig! Something has happened. I heard him cry."

There was no need to answer. The fine fat Easter pig lay prone upon its side, with glazing eyes, and its crimson life-blood stained the snow around.

"Scoundrel!" roared the priest. "You have killed my pig! Oh God! What times are these! That soldier hooligans should come and slay my pig!"

He spoke in the same strain for some moments, bewailing past days and extolling the merits of his pig. Then turning on the dazed couple, he asked angrily, "What are you doing here anyway? Why did you kill my pig?"

The Red Army is fearless in battle, but for once Peter shrank before attack. Marfa came to the rescue.

"It was the Khaldoon," she said simply. "He said the demons would stop our marriage. And we thought . . . that is, your pig frightened our horse. We thought . . . it was a demon. So Peter killed him. Please, Father, forgive us."

The Father's face grew purple. "Killed my pig!" he roared. "Why did you kill my pig? Wretched girl, what means this nonsense of Khaldoons and demons? Why did he kill my pig?"

Then Peter found his voice. "He . . . It . . . was trying to stop our marriage," he said.

"Who? It?" shouted the priest.

"He — the Khaldoon," said Peter. "We thought he had taken the form of a pig."

"Young man," said the priest, gulping down his anger, "I refuse to bandy words with you any longer. You have wantonly destroyed a valuable animal which belongs to me. For that, in due course, if there is justice in this country, you shall pay to the last kopeck. Meanwhile, begone, and leave me in peace."

"But we want you to marry us," said the girl.

Again the priest's face swelled purple. "What!" he thundered, "after this outrageous act you have the impudence to speak to me of marriage? Begone from my sight, you heathen pair, before I curse you. If you were the last people in the world and Gabriel's horn was blowing for the Day of Judgment, and you begged me to marry you, I would say to you as I say now, 'Idolators and murderers, begone!'"

Without a word Peter turned the sleigh and drove back slowly to the village. It seemed that the Red Army had met its Waterloo. Marfa had much to say, and none of it was good hearing to the deflated warrior. She was so utterly right, with the wrong-headed logic of woman, that he could find no words to answer.

Ten years before, a Russian peasant in his place would have sold his horse or his car or his precious store of seed-grain, and paid twenty rubles to the sorcerer.

4

But the Red Army is made of sterner stuff.

To Marfa's surprise her lover drove on past their homes, right on to the village school, which now served as the office for the village soviet. He took her, not roughly, by the shoulder.

"Get out," he said, "and come with me."

"What do you want, Peter?" she asked. "Why have you come here?"

"To get married," he answered grimly. Neither priests nor demons can turn the Red Army from its path.

It was done in five minutes. Peter's clumsy signature, Marfa's cross witnessed by the Registrar, the quick stamp of a seal, and the payment of thirty kopecks. By Soviet law they were husband and wife, till death or divorce should part them.

"Now," said Peter manfully, as he led his bride to the sleigh, "let us hear no more of babies with long black tails."

Marfa said nothing; only squeezed his arm and smiled.

They rode for a while in blissful silence. Then the voice of Eve said plaintively, "But Peterkin, the Khaldoon. . . . Just suppose . . ."

"I shall now deal with the Khaldoon," stated the Red Army. "When I have done with him he will need the help of all his demons. And what is more, I shall tell him that if our baby has as much as one hair on its body, let alone the least vestige of a tail, I will take him and hang him feet upwards to the beam of his own cottage, and light a fire under him and smoke him till his eyes drop out and his body is dry as tinder."

"Oh, Peter, you are wonderful," she cooed. "But . . . but . . . what about the pig?"

"Never mind that," said her young husband, helping her down from the sled. "You go and tell our folks that we are married. They must prepare the feast. I am off to pay a visit to the Khaldoon."

He drew himself up, stretching his muscles, and stroked his broad army belt with its heavy buckle.

5

The Brave Soldier and the Wicked Sorcerer

Some months later the People's Court of the neighboring township was called upon to judge two cases, one for civil damages, the other for assault and battery. In both there was the same defendant, the young soldier Peter Pavlovich Lepatof.

The priest, Timothy Serafimovich Kushkin, brought suit for seventy rubles, the value of a fatted pig, wantonly destroyed by said Peter, for no sufficient motive, with hooliganic intent.

The court after investigation discovered from the owner's admission that the pig had almost reached the term of its career; that, furthermore, its flesh had been utilized by him in a normal manner. It therefore awarded damages of five rubles.

The priest appealed.

The second suit was brought by one Eliphas Antolovich Gourko, demanding a penalty of five hundred rubles for grievous bodily harm inflicted without cause by the defendant, Peter Pavlovich Lepatof, and imprisonment according to the law. Fifteen days, the plaintiff testified, and brought witnesses to support his words, he had been confined to bed as a result of the beating inflicted by Lepatof with a brutal weapon of offense, to wit, a belt of leather with a thick brass buckle. The marks, he declared, he would bear upon his back until he died.

Again the court made full inquiry. It awarded damages of ten rubles. Furthermore, said the verdict, the defendant was condemned to a month's imprisonment, which, in view of his gallant services in the Red Army of the Revolution, should be regarded as conditional.

Like the priest, the sorcerer appealed the case.

It was many months before the suits were tried by the Appeal Court of the provincial capital. The defendant was accompanied by his young wife, who bore on her arm a healthy male child aged seven weeks. In the course of the proceedings, which aroused considerable local interest, the infant, yelling protests, was stripped of its clothing and examined by the court, which pronounced it a perfect specimen of revolutionary youth.

6

The Brave Soldier and the Wicked Sorcerer

Its proud father informed the court that the child had been registered at the village soviet — not christened, he emphasized — under the name of "Reni," an anagram from the Russian words meaning "Revolution the Unique Invention of the People." During its tender years, the parent admitted, the infant would be known by the diminutive "Renka," but when, later, he should be admitted to the Young Pioneers — Communist Boy Scouts — he was to assume the dignity of his full name.

The court listened sympathetically, and congratulated the couple on their blooming babe. Then it proceeded to consider the evidence. After hearing the whole story it gave the following decision.

Whereas: Eliphas Antolovich Gourko, the so-called Khaldoon, had attempted to profit by the lowest form of obsolete superstition, he had received no more than his deserts in the beating administered by the defendant, who had acted in a manner worthy of the Red Army. The previous verdict was therefore set aside. The damages of ten rubles were rescinded, and the month's imprisonment, though conditional, was cancelled. In addition, the plaintiff was warned that the eye of authority was upon him, and that it would go hard with him if he continued his wicked practices.

The case of the priest was considered at greater length. The Court of Appeal realized that in a peasant community the People's Court had been right to stress the importance of property in the form of live stock. After deliberation, it gave the following decision.

"Whereas: it has been shown that the loss to the plaintiff, Timothy Serafimovich Kushkin, resultant from the death of his pig, has been slight, and that he was able to utilize the flesh of said pig in the accustomed manner, the Court of Appeal decides that the verdict of five rubles damages to be paid by the defendant is maintained. But insomuch as the priest showed anger and spoke words incompatible with the tenets of the religious office he professes to administer, and, furthermore, for purely personal reasons of malice and revenge refused in the most categorical manner to carry out the duties imposed upon him by said office, he is hereby condemned to pay a fine of twenty rubles to the village soviet, to be employed for educational purposes as the soviet may see fit."

Witch of the Alcazar

LUIS RODRIGAS dared not breathe as the guard held the paper close to the smoky lamp. It was cold in the vault of the gateway and the walls were damp.

"It looks all right," said the guard sulkily, "but you're late, comrade; it's nearly midnight. The other boys from Valencia got here hours ago."

"The Fascists attacked us. I was cut off with four others who were killed; one died in my arms; he worked in the same shop with me. Look, my tunic's still wet with his blood." He spoke in the sing-song Valencian accent he had learned from his father's stable-boys. Surely that would fool him as it had fooled them on the truck.

"Yes," Luis went on, "and see the hole here. An inch nearer and I'd be lying out there beside him. But I couldn't leave him before he died; he was my best friend. Afterward — it was dark, but a truck gave me a lift from Maqueda."

"All right," said the other; "go ahead."

Luis raised his left fist, "*Salud*," and held himself to a weary shuffle along the darkened street. Inside Toledo at last, his heart exulted, though he walked in a dead man's shoes and wore a dead man's clothing.

He breathed thanks to his name saint, and instinctively his hand went to his throat, to the little silver cross he had worn round his neck since baptism. It wasn't there, and for an instant he stopped in horror, then remembered and patted the cartridge belt — shotgun cartridges at that — did they think to meet rifles with shotguns? Yes, the cross was here in the third one, with the message from the colonel. They had made him take it off before he started. "Your scarf might slip and they'd see the chain. Those priest-killers don't wear crosses, and your job's risky enough as it is."

The colonel didn't want to let him go, but the news was bad, the Alcazar might fall any day. Small wonder, after eight weeks' siege or more. They said it had fallen three days ago after the big explosion, but the firing began again, so that was a lie, thank God. There'd been twenty volunteers to take the message that rescue was coming, but none of them could imitate the popular dialect as he could. Then, too, he knew Toledo and could find his way through it at night.

Strange how little he'd cared when they'd stripped the dead man's clothes off and he had put them on. Almost the same age they were — the paper said nineteen and he would be twenty at Christmas. But he did mind taking off the cross. It was not the same to have it in the cartridge at his belt.

He turned to the left into an alley so narrow that no cart could pass. It was dark as a tunnel, for the upper stories of the buildings on either side hung over it so close that their windows almost touched. Every forty yards an oil lamp flickered feebly. Luis shivered as he stumbled over the rough cobblestones; the cloth was wet over his chest and the thick canvas shoes scraped his bare feet.

He felt terribly alone in this hostile city. A sudden burst of machine-gun fire made him jump and cower against the wall, although he knew that it was far on the hillside above him. If only he could hurry, but that was impossible in these winding alleys.

With a sigh of relief he came out on a little square halfway up the hillside where a group of soldiers sat drinking round a charcoal brazier whose glow was hidden from enemy aircraft by a tall umbrella.

"*Salud*, comrade," shouted a tipsy voice. "Have a drink; we've got plenty."

10

He caught the Catalan accent and went on boldly. There were six of them, but two, he saw, were women with the same red-and-black caps and scarfs and blue denim tunics as the men. Enemies or not, Luis was glad of their company and the warmth and the strong red wine. Cautiously he drew from them news of the Alcazar. There was a breach in the wall, one told him. "We could rush it," he added boastfully, "but this lot from Madrid wants all the glory for themselves, and they don't dare to try it. How long will they wait? Let them rush it now, I say, or give Barcelona a chance."

The others echoed him in rougher terms; clearly there was no love lost between Barcelona and Madrid, but as a Valencian they made him welcome. They pressed him to stay when he rose to leave them, but he said no, he must report back to his comrades; they probably thought him dead. He felt more cheerful as he went on from the square into the maze of alleys. Once he thought he was lost; there should have been a turn to the left which would bring him almost to the north wall of the Alcazar, where the Catalans had said the breach was made, but the passage went on without a break on either side.

As he felt his way slowly forward, a ghastly scream behind him checked him like a blow, and he felt the hair bristle on the back of his neck. As he darted for the wall there was a scuffle of bodies at his feet and the familiar fury of fighting cats. He leaned there trembling, hardly able to stand, then grabbed his gun tightly and went on with quivering nerves. What a fool he was to be thus startled but always he had hated cats from childhood. At last here was the passage, narrow as the others but clear open to the sky. He breathed deeply; now he knew where he was, he was skirting the lowest wall of the Alcazar. Two hundred yards farther, if the Catalans had told the truth, the breach began with open ground in front of it. The alley wound along the hillside, the river was not far below.

When he came to the open space, he lay flat on the ground and

11

put his gun down quietly. There was more light here and his eyes were accustomed to the darkness. Would there be Red sentries? He crawled forward inch by inch — there was no sign of a living thing. As he stared at the mound of rubble that towered above him, he realized that the hardest part of his enterprise was yet to come. Somehow all of them, he and the others, had taken for granted that if only he could win his way to the Alcazar his task was ended. But how to communicate with the defenders, and was it possible to scale the breach without making noise that would bring a burst of fire from friends and enemies alike? There must be Reds in the houses below him, under cover no doubt, but alert. He crawled to the right where the supports of the northwest tower were a mass of crumbled masonry. Perhaps here?

Suddenly the earth rose under him and flung him backward amidst a din of shattering noise and falling stones. He felt himself whirled through the air. Faster than light his brain flashed, "Will I fall in the river?" Then blackness swallowed him.

"Let me alone, I'm tired," he muttered. "I want to sleep."

The hand on his breast shook him again. "Can you stand?" a voice whispered. "Come on, you can't stay here. Drink this."

His head was raised and he felt a tin cup clink against his teeth, and gasped as the fiery spirit burned his mouth. That roused him and he sat up and tried to stand, but fell on hands and knees.

"All right then, crawl; I'll help you," said the voice and, half crawling, half dragged, Luis followed down a narrow passage and lay exhausted on a flagged courtyard. A moment later the glow of a small oil lamp showed a dark figure in militia uniform standing by the little fountain in a courtyard.

"What happened?" Luis asked weakly.

"A mine exploded and I ran out afterward and found you," came the low reply. "You fell right at my door. Here, take more of this."

He drank the cupful and the blood flowed hot through his veins. He sat up and looked about him. His head hurt horribly and he

12

ached all over, but he could move his arms and legs and seemed to have no wound. He drew a deep breath. "I remember," he said. "I remember. Give me some more brandy."

His eyes were clearer now and, as the dark figure moved to take the cup, he stared in surprise. It was a woman, a tall girl with a pale face and dark hair cut short at the neck. She wore the blue tunic of the militia and a red-and-black anarchist scarf.

"Can you stand?" she asked. "Here, lean on me; this way."

Holding the lamp before her she led him to a corner and opened a narrow door. "Wait," he muttered. "I don't — it smells of cats."

She took no notice. "Look out; there are two steps here," she said. "Now, this way to the right. Mind your head, the beams are low. There, that's it." She opened another door and helped him to a couch against the wall. "Sit there," she said, "while I light the other lamp. That's better. Wait, I'll be back in a minute."

Luis was in a small room from the center of whose vaulted roof hung an old bronze lamp. There was a rug on the stone floor and the couch on which he lay was clean, although its woodwork was black with age. Opposite him embers glowed in a deep, open fireplace. To his left was a carved oak cupboard and beside it a window shuttered and sealed.

The girl came back with pillows and blankets and a bowl of hot water. "Lie down," she said, "and let's have a look at you. And pull off your jacket while I untie your shoes. Don't be silly," as he hesitated, "I'm a trained nurse, and I've got to look at you." She helped him strip and turned him over. "It's all right," she said as he flinched when her fingers pressed his shoulder. "You were lucky, I tell you. It's a bad bruise and another here on your hip, but there's nothing broken. You'll be all right again tomorrow."

She washed his cuts and rubbed them with ointment that smarted, then covered him with a blanket. "Lie still while I get soup. I tell you, you're a lucky one."

13

Witch of the Alcazar

The brandy was singing in his head and the pain was dulled. Half dazed, he gulped the soup she brought him and ate the bread.

"There, now you'll sleep," she said softly, "and sleep will make you well. Go to sleep, now sleep."

The light was lowered and he felt her hand cool and soothing on his forehead. "Sleep," she murmured, "sleep." . . .

When Luis woke the fire had been replenished and was burning brightly. On a little table by the couch there was a pitcher of wine and a plate with bread and cold chicken. Attached to the bread by a knife was a piece of paper with writing on it. His head was clear and he felt no pain, but as soon as he tried to move every limb and muscle groaned protest — he was as sore as if he'd been beaten all over. He rubbed himself vigorously and the stiffness lessened, then he got out of bed, picked up the paper and held it to the firelight. The writing was strange and angular and the ink was very black. "Eat your breakfast," the note said. "You will find everything you want. I will be back at twelve."

In the corner by the cupboard he saw a washstand with towels, but he looked in vain for his clothes. He walked gingerly to the door — each step was painful — and turned the handle. It was locked. He stared at it stupidly — a thick oak door backed with iron. He shrugged his shoulders and sat down on the couch and ate ravenously. The wine was rough and bitter, but he was thirsty and drank it all.

Only a few minutes after he had washed, the door opened and the girl came in. She seemed very tall in the leaping firelight, taller than he, with broad shoulders, walking with a swing like a man, and the double peaks of her red-and-black cap were so big they looked like horns.

"You're awake," she said. "That's good. How do you feel?"

"I'm all right," said Luis. "I was awfully stiff at first, but it's better now." He paused and added, "I want to thank you; I think you saved my life."

14

She smiled and came closer to the couch. Her lips were very red and her teeth were white, and her eyes shone strangely in the firelight, now red, now green.

"I was glad to do it," she said simply. "Let me look at your shoulder. Wait, I'll light the lamp. Yes," she said slowly, "all black and blue, and so's your hip, but it doesn't matter. Those trifling cuts are nothing and there isn't a mark on your chest, and your skin is lovely and white."

Her fingers scarcely touched him but his flesh tingled, and he did not like the note of appraisal in her voice. Did she think . . . He pulled the blanket up to his chin and leaned on his elbow facing her.

"I must go," he said; "I must report to my column. Where is my uniform?"

She watched him without answer. By God, he had been right before, her eyes *were* green. She did not meet his gaze but looked down at the table between them, at the plate and the empty wine jug.

"You want to leave me," she said, "though you say I saved your life. Oh, no, you must not leave me. Soon, I think, you will not want to leave me." Her voice was gentle and her mouth was smiling, but something made Luis clutch at his neck beneath the blanket for the cross that was not there. He moistened his lips with his tongue and said firmly, "I must go; it's my duty. If you will not bring my clothes, I shall go and look for them myself."

"Do not trouble, I will bring them; but when I have brought them I do not think you'll want to go."

She went quickly to the other room and a moment later was back with his clothes and shoes. She dropped them in front of her and stood with her back against the door. "Come and get them," she said. "I have served you enough. And don't be shy; I saw you naked last night. Come quickly, why don't you move?"

15

Witch of the Alcazar

Why didn't he move? His brain said move, but his body wouldn't obey. He could not move.

The woman laughed lightly. She picked up the clothes and put them on the end of the couch and stood again near the door. His forehead was wet with the effort of will to make his limbs obey, but he couldn't move. "What have you done?" he cried in a strangled voice. "Have you bewitched me?"

She smiled. "You asked for your clothes and I told you that if I brought them you wouldn't want to go. If you want to, rise and take them; if you don't, you'd sooner stay. I thought you would. Then stay and sleep awhile, but I must leave you, for I have much to do. And if you really want to go, get up and dress and go your way."

With a swift, feline movement she put out the lamp. Then she turned and left the room. The door closed but no key clicked in the lock, no bolt was drawn.

Luis lay, weak with panic. What did this mean? His body was powerless but his mind whirled madly through his head like a squirrel in its cage. Was he hypnotized? No, that was impossible. Yet she had said — Suddenly he recalled the bitter taste of the wine and the woman's glance at the empty pitcher. Yes, that was it; he was poisoned. But such poison he had never heard of, to bind his limbs yet leave him free to think and speak. What did it mean? What was there — who had said — where had he heard — ? In agony he struggled to recapture the old memory which escaped him. There was something — if only —

Firelight — firelight — the woman's green eyes in the firelight, and the cap with its peaks like horns. Yes, that was it; now the memory was coming. What memory — what horns? He fought to think farther, but his eyes were closing, he must sleep.

A sound of singing roused him. The room was brightly lighted and at first his eyes were dazzled. He tried to move but the paralysis

16

still held him. Beside his couch stood four tall figures, two by two, carrying a litter. They wore long black robes embroidered with red symbols, and their heads were hidden by the high-peaked cowl donned by servants of the Inquisition when heretics were burned in the auto-da-fé. As the chant rose Luis could distinguish words: "The hour of the Sabbath approaches — the midnight hour is near — to the house of Illian our founder — the victim was sent by the Master — the victim was sent but came willing — he came to our door as is fitting — the victim is fair without blemish." The music swelled louder, and the singing changed to an unknown jargon of rolling polysyllables.

Luis had heard enough. The words "Sabbath" and "Illian" had unlocked his childish memory of his old nurse with her tales of sorcery — of Illian, the Wizard of Toledo, and of the witches' Sabbath. Yes, and of the extract of a poisonous fruit, with which the victims were made ready — awake and fully conscious, unable to move but alive to feel and suffer.

The chant ended and they laid him on the litter, resistless as a corpse, then carried him in silence out across the little courtyard and down a sloping passage on the farther side. His bearers halted and he heard the rustle of a curtain drawn aside, and as they went on, the closing of a door. Again the unknown chant, this time from a choir of voices close at hand.

They laid the litter down and raised him in their arms up to a monstrous Thing, which stood there with arms outstretched, black and shaggy, taller than a bear from pointed hoofs to the crimson face, inhuman in its lineaments of hate and lustful grin and sprouting horns above the broad red forehead. This was the Ancient Evil, the Devil-Goat, Anti-Christ, the Unclean Thing.

They placed him sitting on the outstretched arms and laid his head back, gently, against the hairy breast.

"Shall we bind him?" he heard a whisper. "The datura wears off quickly from the young and strong."

17

"No need," came the reply. "We must hurry, the time is short, and the end will be soon."

Luis closed his eyes, half-fainting, and the music rose to a crescendo, followed by utter silence. Then a wild sound of movement and excited cries.

When he looked again, hope flooded him for a moment. This could not be true; it was a nightmare, not real, and soon he would wake to safety. Before him in a large hectagonal room moved a line of dancers like a gigantic snake, turning on itself and weaving in fantastic measures. There must have been twoscore of them, leaping high in the air with bestial cries, but always holding to the snake formation and keeping time to the beat of the drums. Were they human or animal? He could not tell. Or demons from the Pit, these goats and she-wolves and devils with tails and horns? The leader was a giant lynx, black as ebony, with two great pointed ears erect above its head. In a swirl of movement the head and tail of the serpent came together and joined hands, and instantly the whole company formed a circle, in a furious gallop to wild czardas music. Faster and faster they rushed until Luis saw nothing save a whirl of color. Then a clash of cymbals and the circle halted.

No, it was not a dream. No dream could counterfeit the horrid animal reek that filled the room. Luis gasped convulsively as the cat-leader leaped out to the middle of the floor holding high a living toad and began a hideous parody of the words men had held most sacred for two thousand years, then tore the toad in pieces with steely claws and scattered the fragments in the air.

Horror-stricken by the blasphemy, Luis tried to cross himself, and though the gesture failed, his hand had moved six inches. He set his teeth and shut his eyes to hide the dreadful scene, but he could not close his ears to the words which froze his blood. Suddenly the cat smell was rank in his nostrils. Despite himself he must

18

look. The Creature stood before him. Its mouth and chin were human but the eyes in the furry mask above were oblique and green as any cat's. Again he saw the gleam of claws as they struck and scored his breast on either side from shoulder down to waist.

The Creature gave a fearful yowl which the others echoed. Then it leaped back and began a high-pitched gabble in the unknown tongue. The pain spurred Luis' nerves; he clenched his fists and felt that his muscles would obey him. The effect of the drug was passing.

As the gabble ceased, a demon sprang out from the watching circle with a short curved knife. The cat seized it and crouched as if to spring, when with a thunderous crash the roof split open in a hail of flying stones and red-hot metal. A shell fragment flew buzzing over Luis' head and struck the grinning mouth above him with a shock that hurled the demon statue sideways. As it fell Luis leaped clear and stood swaying and shaking but master of his strength. All the lamps save one were extinguished, and the room was a shambles of shrieks and writhing bodies.

A group of survivors was battering at the door. It swung outward and they surged up the passage in a frenzied *sauve qui peut*, heedless of Luis at their heels. Across the courtyard they rushed, along the passage and out into the space below the fortress wall, like fiends spewed forth from hell.

Instantly men were among them, leaping down from the fortress wall, stabbing and shooting. "*Arriba España!*" they shouted. "For God and our Country."

"*Arriba España!*" cried Luis with the last rush of his ebbing strength. "*Arriba España* — friends — I bring news —"

They caught him as he fell, and he heard the sharp report of pistols and the crash of grenades. Then a word of command: "Back to the breach. They've had their lesson. Bring this one with us. Friend or prisoner, we'll know later."

19

He knew he was lifted, felt stones rolling as they climbed, then everything went black.

This story was told me by one of the American correspondents with Franco's army, who was the first foreigner to talk with the Alcazar survivors. He said he heard it from a young cadet who took part in the sortie which rescued Rodrigas.

"Did you write it?" I asked.

"Of course not; I didn't believe it," he replied.

"Do you always believe what you write?" I murmured.

He grinned. "You go to hell. . . . But this was too fantastic — even for our crowd."

I thought so too, although I happened to know that Michelet in his book on witches speaks of the *hennin*, or forage cap with two high peaks, as being the ritual headgear of the "priestess" at the "Sabbath." I also knew that the famous Toledo wizard, Illian, is said to have lived in a narrow alley at the foot of the Alcazar.

However, I thought no more about it until some weeks later in London when I saw an English doctor whom I had met in Barcelona with a Red Cross unit working for the Loyalists. He said that he had been captured in Toledo by the Rebels but fortunately one of their surgeons had recognized him, and that before being sent home he had helped to take care of the wounded from the Alcazar.

"They were gallant fellows," he said, "but there was some exaggeration about their sufferings. I saw few that were seriously undernourished and many of the wounds were contusions of no graver character than caused by falling stones. There was one case, though," he added, "which I must say puzzled me. It was a wound all right, but in four years' experience in France I never saw anything like it. He was a young man about twenty, I suppose one of the cadets, although I was too busy to ask him, and my Spanish isn't good. It was the most curious thing you ever saw. On each side of his chest, from the top right down to the waist, were five parallel

20

cuts, not deep but in rather a messy state through lack of treatment. I suppose they were made with a sharpened rake or some such implement. You know some of those poor devils of militia had no proper arms, just blunderbusses or scythes and mattocks. Yes, it must have been a rake."

The Village Maiden
and the Three Bad Boys

THE MOSAIC LAW, as given in Deuteronomy, guarded jealously the virtue of the women of Israel. Many of them worked on the land, far from help. A harsh penalty was decreed if the wrongful act was done in a field, because perchance "the damsel cried, and there was none to save her."

Laws die and prophets pass, but sowing and reaping go on unchanged. Still young men and maidens set out together to the harvest, and play their parts in Life beneath the sun. And still judges and courts must deal with sins as old as earth.

The Soviet, ruling wide and fertile plains, makes laws to save the women of Russia from offence. In its war upon "hooliganism," — youthful violence and depravity — crimes of this kind have been punished by death.

But the hand of justice sometimes slips, as it may have done in those other days, when the Law of Moses was still new.

One summer day Anna Petrovna, a village girl of good reputation, went to work in the fields. In the evening she came home tearful to her father, Peter Petrovich, and said she had been mistreated by three of the village boys, Boris, Ivan and Pavel.

In wrath her father, a poor landless peasant, ran to the county town and made complaint to the police. The trial was set for a date two months later, after the harvest, for nothing short of murder can interfere with the business of bringing in the grain. As all three culprits were sons of prosperous peasants, well known in the community, they were not arrested or imprisoned, but were put in

22

charge of the village soviet, to be brought to judgment on the day appointed.

Before a week had passed Boris, with his father, drove up to the cottage of Peter Petrovich. He met them with solemn face. His heart, he said, was broken, his one ewe lamb besmirched.

Boris blubbered, and his father took up the tale. Boris, he admitted, had behaved in a brutal and unseemly manner, but youth was youth; and blood ran hot in the summer; and a pretty girl — he waved his hand — "We have been young and foolish ourselves, Peter Petrovich. Would you send this poor boy to prison for years, for a fault so natural to his age?"

The injured parent was stern. That was exactly what he wished to do, he said. As for the follies of youth, his guest could speak for himself. All the world knew that rich men could pay for their pleasures; to a poor peasant like himself life was harder. Even in his rawest years he would never have done such a thing.

The visitor changed his tone. He understood that, he said. He, for his part, and his unworthy son — he threw a dark look at the tearful Boris — were willing to make amends. Let Peter Petrovich also consider the matter. Perhaps it could be arranged.

On that the interview ended, with expressions of mutual respect.

A few days later Ivan came, with his brother Sergey, a battalion commander in the Red Army. The soldier took a man-of-the-world tone and came to the point with military promptness. Ivan had behaved disgracefully, there was no doubt about it. In the army he would probably have been shot. But, amongst fellow-villagers, why make a painful scene? Surely the matter could be arranged. Of course it was not a question of money, but perhaps he and Peter Petrovich could put their heads together. . . . Meanwhile let the latter think it over once more.

The visit ended, one might almost say, with cordiality.

Last came Pavel, guided by his mother, the richest widow in the county. Her husband had been killed by the Whites for refusing to

The Village Maiden and the Three Bad Boys

show them a ford across the river, to strike at the Red Army. In recognition of this, his family had been allowed to keep their big farm, which otherwise would have been seized and redistributed by the village soviet.

To Peter Petrovich's surprise, the widow flung herself upon him weeping. She begged him to take pity on a tortured mother's heart. Recovering, he said with dignity, "Marfa Timofeyevna, I too am a parent. Do you think my heart does not bleed for my poor anguished child?"

The widow tried again. She knew, she said, the depth of Peter Petrovich's sorrow. But why make bad blood out of it all? The evil deed of which her son was guilty could never be undone, but could not youth's errors be repaired? Surely something might be arranged.

The visit ended without rancor, and again Peter Petrovich was left to think it over.

Russian peasants are vengeful, it is said, but they are also shrewd. From the beginning Peter Petrovich had seen his way. The questions in his mind were only how much he could safely ask, how little accept without loss of face. He pondered long, and took counsel with his cronies.

Then he summoned the relatives of the three young men to visit his humble cottage. The boys, he said, were guilty, and the court's sentence was bound to be severe. But prison years are long and bleak, walled off from the fields and sunshine. Nor would that help his daughter.

Suppose, however, — he paused and eyed them slyly — suppose, on certain conditions — suppose, when the case came to trial, the girl should withdraw something and hint that fear of him, her father, had led her to exaggerate; that she had been, in fact, less sinned against than she had said. Why should the court not believe her? The boys would say the same. And so, in that event (his smile was crafty) much trouble might be avoided.

His three visitors exchanged looks of relief.

24

The Village Maiden and the Three Bad Boys

Yes, they said, that would avoid much trouble. But . . . what were the conditions of which Peter Petrovich spoke?

The peasant stroked his beard, watching each of them in turn. This was the crux of the question.

It was hard, he declared, for a father to condone an offence like this. All three young men were guilty and should be punished, but it was his daughter's welfare that he thought of rather than revenge.

Again he hesitated, then poured it all out at once. Let one of them marry the girl, a second provide house and land, and the third bring implements for the farm, seed, grain and stock, a horse and buggy, furniture and a feather mattress. On that basis, perhaps, something might be arranged.

The families of the three boys met this offer with anger and reproach. Did Peter Petrovich think his daughter was a princess, they asked, that she should have a husband and a dowry and a house and farm, all given free, for the act of a summer's eve?

But the old man held the whip-hand. The People's Court of the Soviet Republic did not look lightly on acts like these, he said. Nowadays the daughter of the poorest peasant could get justice, even from rich *kulaks'* sons.

The three families realized with pain that this was true. The very social differences that made his terms so distasteful would prove their ruin if the charge was pressed. After much delay and bargaining, they accepted Peter Perovich's offer.

Each of the three young men offered himself as husband. After all the girl was strong and comely, and house and farm and stock and furniture cost money.

Peter Petrovich was puzzled, but his problem was solved by Anna, who vowed that Boris was the only one she would dream of marrying. Let the others fix their shares as they would.

And thus it was arranged.

Pavel's mother resentfully allotted ten acres from her holding and agreed to build the house. The Red Army Commander promised seed-grain and implements and stock and furniture. They had no choice.

Who now so happy as Peter Petrovich who saw himself risen to power in the village, father-in-law of a prosperous youth, patron of two others! Never had he hoped for so rich a marriage for his daughter. Loudly he thanked God for the Revolution and its protection of the poor.

The case came up for trial. The boys pleaded not guilty, and Anna Petrovna, blushing, admitted that she might have exaggerated in telling the story to her father. It was a hot day, and they had worked hard. They were old friends. She had thought a little drink would do no harm. So they drank beer mixed with vodka, and afterwards — she looked down — well, afterwards . . . she might have been a silly girl. . . . She was sorry she had deceived her father, but she had been afraid. He was so strict about boys. And . . . she sobbed into her handkerchief.

The People's Court spoke a few sharp words about the evils of alcohol and gave a reminder that all three youths would be held liable for the support of the child, if there should be one.

The case was then dismissed.

On the following Sunday Peter Petrovich, in his best, walked to the home of his prospective son-in-law to talk over plans for the wedding. To his horror the widow said that she did not know what he meant. Her son had been acquitted, she reminded him. Neither he nor his daughter had any claim on her.

"But you agreed," he stammered, "you agreed that Boris should marry her."

"Have we signed a paper?" asked the widow. "Have you any proof of what you say? Not one scrap. Go then about your way and leave us in peace."

Tearing his beard and cursing, Peter shuffled homewards. Why had he been afraid to put the bargain upon paper? Was it possible that they would cheat him thus?

The Village Maiden and the Three Bad Boys

There was still hope that the other two families would be more loyal than the grasping widow. He turned about and hurried to visit them. In vain. They were leagued against him. No one would fulfil the pledge.

Desperate he went once more to the People's Court and told his story. To his bewilderment he was treated with contumely. An unnatural father, the court called him, who had sought to profit by his daughter's shame. What was more, he was himself a criminal. He had compounded a felony and was liable to punishment. Instead of going to prison for a term of years he would be let off this time with a warning in view of his ignorance and humble station, but in future let him be very careful.

For Peter Petrovich it was cruel; one day puffed with pride, dreaming of wealth, the morrow a criminal, an unnatural father, hopeless and forlorn. Like a dog that has lost his master he ran to and fro, weeping and begging for advice. He was given mockery often, sympathy sometimes, but never help or redress.

At last he went to the town and sought a letter-writer famed throughout the region. On fair white paper he bade the scribe set down the following letter to Mikhail Ivanovich Kalinin, Peasant President of all the Socialist Republics of all the Soviets:

"O Comrade President, I cry to you in my distress, for I know that you have a feeling heart, ever warm towards the sorrows of the poor. You yourself, Your Greatness, were once a small peasant such as I, and you will understand the sad story I tell."

He gave the facts at length, and ended: "You understand such things as these, and you will see that I have acted rightly, that I have done as any father would. They tell me that I have broken the law and should be punished. In truth it is these boys who did wrong by my daughter who should be punished. Yet why should I be harsh and send them to prison? That would not help my girl. I took the right way. It would have been better that one should marry her, another give the house and farm, the third the goods they need.

27

"And now they mock me and my daughter with talk of signed papers. And the People's Court speaks always of my sin and never of the boys' sin.

"Is there no justice, Comrade President? I beg and pray you to send forthwith a message ordering that these false ones be held to their bargain, or punished for their crime."

It came to my knowledge that Kalinin was moved by this appeal and wished to help Peter Petrovich, but there was nothing he could do. The letter of Law is not always the Spirit of Justice.

The Gold Train

I FOUND MYSELF one night in a third-class compartment in Siberia — traveling *hard* they call it, and hard means hard in Siberia. The Russians are a hardy race and they must be to travel hard in Siberia, but you meet a lot more people when you travel hard. And their piles of baggage and sacks of potatoes and bundles and bedding, and their fleas and bugs and lice and probably cockroaches, and cats and dogs and hens and goats and sometimes calves as well and little pigs, and always babies. If Herod had ever traveled hard in Siberia he'd have killed more babies than he did. That's what traveling hard means. Yet, by myself in a Wagon-lits coupé I should never have known the truth of the end of Kolchak's gold train.

It began with a woman nursing her child, which howled like a wolf for its milk, and when she gave it her breast it wouldn't just drink and shut up but kicked and kicked and wriggled, and kicked a thin gold chain with a thick gold coin on it out for the world to see. That made her blush and she smacked the child and tucked the coin away, with a quick, nervous gesture, and the child was sick, and altogether it was a touching domestic scene until the baby went to sleep and I managed to get her to talk. It wasn't easy but I managed it . . . that's a reporter's business. They don't always tell you the truth, but this sounded like truth, and I had seen the coin. It was an American twenty-dollar gold piece.

She said, this woman did, that she was a daughter of a *Kulak*, the type of prosperous peasant that used to be admired by authority and called the backbone of the country, the way they do with hon-

29

est yeomen in England and farmers in America, especially when votes are needed. They didn't need votes in Russia, not in Czarist Russia, but they did need soldiers and tough Cossacks to suppress the proletariat. Which the Kulaks, it seems, were always willing to do, because the word Kulak means fist: to punch their poorer neighbors in the eye, or squeeze them in bony fingers till the juice ran out. Exactly as the Bolsheviks have recently squeezed the Kulaks.

This Kulak, the woman's father, was a hard and greedy Kulak, in the days before the war, when she was a lovely slim girl, with hair like ripe wheat, and a lover named Ivan Petrovich, who was a *Batrak*, which means the poorest kind of peasant, without a cent and never an inch of land and nothing in the world save the love of the Kulak's daughter, who loved him more than all the world.

But Ivan Petrovich was brave, like a dog of good blood, she said, against a bear. And he faced the old bear of a Kulak, and the Kulak laughed and said, "Love, you say, love. Do men eat love? Do cows eat love? Not even pigs eat love. You love my daughter; you want her. All right then, boy, you can take her when you bring me fifty golden pieces of ten roubles each. Then you can take her and welcome and that's a fair offer, the same as I made this morning to the son of my neighbor the innkeeper. Five hundred roubles in gold and the girl is yours. Or his. And that's my last word," said the cruel, grasping Kulak, and neither frowned nor smiled as he said it, and his eyes were cold. Cold as gold pieces that have lain all night on the Siberian snow.

Swift and sudden as lightning in August, the war then came and took both her suitors — Ivan the poor and Vasya the rich. And more than once her father would have wed her to another, but she held him to his word, and who should be so mad as to give fifty golden pieces for one young girl in any Siberian village? Months passed and years, and in the third summer a man limped home on a

30

wooden stump, with the voice of a crow and a rattle in his lungs. He had breathed yellow smoke, he said, that burned like flame, and they had cut his foot off; but he did not want to die so far from home.

He gave the girl a ring of copper with a rough-shaped heart of lead in the center, and told her Ivan Petrovich had made it from a bullet that pierced his shoulder: made it for her from the bullet that pierced his body, and sent with it a message — the first words he had learned to write: "I sEnd yoU thiS in ToKen oF The WorD yoU pLedGed mE iVAn PETrovicH." "Is he dead?" she cried, and the man coughed and choked and couldn't answer. She thought of that last night, when they met that last time and exchanged vows of love forever: when she told him she was his, only his till death; and Death himself should have her before another man should wed her. Then the soldier with gas in his lungs croaked weakly, "Oh, no, he got well and went back to the war and sends you this ring and this message, and bids you wait and hope."

Now there were tidings of revolt in cities and landlords' houses burning; and red flags in neighboring Irkutsk, and fighting on the railroad: and a new soviet in the village to replace the old council of elders. The members were the same, except for the priest, who hid himself, but their emblem was sickle and hammer instead of double eagle. Until the Whites came back and the double eagle came back. Then they hid the red flags and the sickle and hammer, and the priest came forth from hiding. And foreign soldiers came, and Red partisans came, and they fought to and fro. The peasants hid their cattle in the forest and changed sides when needful, and trafficked and robbed, and were robbed and beaten, never knowing what it was all about, nor caring much; with only one wish that someone would win outright, or that all of them would kill one another and leave the land in peace.

One autumn noon a boy brought word from Ivan Petrovich, her

31

lover, to meet him at dusk by the river with food and tobacco and linen and drink. There were five of them there — Red soldiers, spent and beaten. Two were wounded, but Ivan was brown and well, a Red commander with a red star on his breast. They were running now, he told her; his patrol was betrayed and ambushed; but soon they would return in force. He knew the Whites were breaking. Soon, he said, the war would end, and he would come to claim her. But he only laughed when she spoke of the fifty gold pieces. And she was sad and frightened, since she greatly feared her father, who was harder and colder than ever and now chairman of the council of elders, or alternately president of the village soviet.

Ivan fled that night, and the war went on and autumn froze into winter, and the peasants buried their grain and hid their cattle and goods. Until an icy dawn when the roaring of cannon aroused them in terror, and shells fell among their houses, to explode like thunder and lightning. They ran to the woods distraught, all scattered like sheep when a wolf raids the flock and the shepherd is gone. The girl found herself alone in a thicket on top of a hill, breathless and bruised. Her clothing was torn and she lay on the ground, when a sudden loud shouting below to the right spurred her panic afresh. But the shells had ceased, the shells that had frightened her, and she was a daughter of Eve, so she crept through the bushes to look — and witnessed the fabulous end of the treasure convoy of the beaten White leader, Admiral Kolchak.

Not twenty yards below her hiding place stood the train with its huge engine, and a mob of soldiers was milling around a closed steel car. Then one climbed up with a bag in his hand, which he tied to the door bolt, and dropped like a stone and tried to crawl under the car. The rest turned to run and tripped one another, plunging and fighting. Their voices rose shrill, like the crying of wounded hares. The grenades exploded and the steel door lurched forward down on the mass of them. Like a cascade of yellow wheat, from the broken boxes, gold flooded over them — a cascade of gold whose drops

32

were coins, flooded and drowned them in waves of gold and their own blood.

Others came rushing like ants and crawled onto the golden heap, filling their pockets and blouses and boots with handfuls of shining coins, rushing and crawling like ants on a heap of golden grain, mad with their greed for gold, clasping it close in their arms, holding it close to their hearts, clasping their hearts' desire. Then a clatter of bullets rang the steel sides of the treasure car as the Red machine guns opened fire.

That sobered them, most of them, though not all of them. Most of them ran before the range was corrected, and those who stayed were cut by the scythe of bullets like poppies in a wheatfield. The gold heap shone bright in the early sun, yellow and red like wheat and poppies, gold and blood. The looters ran with their gold, ran for life and their golden booty. One made for the hill where the girl was hiding and tried to climb, but the weight of the gold dragged him back and he slipped to the bottom. He climbed up again, halfway, and the eyes stood forth from his head, and a bullet found him as he clung panting to the frozen soil, and he rolled to the bottom, dead. The others were lurching now, as they lumbered across the fields. The lucky ones lurched the most, the lucky ones who had the most gold to fill their pockets and blouses and boots with dead weight. The Reds on ponies rode them down, shouting with laughter. They lurched and staggered like drunken men, and one sat down and pulled off his boot, and the coins sprayed out like yellow flame in the sunlight. The nearest Red gave a shout, and the man jumped up and ran, dot and go one, dot and go one, across the frozen stubble till his bare foot was bloody. The Reds laughed so much they missed every shot, and the man won on to a ditch at the edge of the wood and gathered himself for a leap, one leap to shelter, then stopped and jerked back and fell headlong as the bullet struck. The Reds rode on shouting with laughter.

33

The Gold Train

The girl watched it without sound, scarcely breathing. Was it real, or a nightmare of fear and wealth, a dream of longing for her lover and fear that he might die, might be killed in the war, might never come back? Days and nights of fear, weeks and months and years of fear, with the memory of her father's cold eyes and the fifty pieces of gold, the price he had set for her. "Bring them, Ivan Petrovich, and the girl is yours." No, it was not a dream and she could not wake.

He was not dead, the man in the ditch; he was crawling up to the wood. Slow as a snake with a broken back he wriggled out of the ditch and lay on the snow at the edge of the wood, and a small red stain spread out at his side. With an effort he caught at his boot and tugged at it, heel and toe, and off it came with its golden spray, and the man fell back and beat with his hands a moment or two and jerked like a frog, and lay still. So then she went home like one in a dream.

Two days later Ivan rode into the village with his Red detachment. "Kolchak is dead," they shouted. "They tried and shot him in Irkutsk, and the war is over."

Ivan came to claim his girl while her father was out at a meeting. (Do you remember that he was president of the village soviet?) "Have you brought the gold," she asked him, "the fifty pieces my father told you?" He laughed and said, "The war is over; there is no more use for gold in Russia." He was wrong, of course, twice wrong: the war was far from over, and gold is useful many years later, in the Union of Soviet Socialist Republics. She replied, smiling slyly, "Wilt thou steal me from my father? He's a hard man, but his heart is Red . . . and he is president of the soviet which your army is sworn to protect, Ivanusha my beloved." And Ivan cursed her father and cursed the village soviet, but he could not curse the oath he had sworn to the Red army.

"Of course I have no money," he shouted. "I shall take you without money." She smiled again and said, "There is no need, the

34

debt is paid." Then she told him of the gold train, and the hunting and the slaughter, and the barefoot man who gained the wood and died. "He was lying there next morning; there were fifty coins beside him, so cold they burned my fingers when I picked them off the snow. Just fifty and one great one, one strange one, which I kept. (See, it's here around my neck on Mother's chain, but now it's warm.) So I took the fifty pieces, golden pieces each of ten roubles, and gave them to my father in thy name. I gave him too thy message on the crumpled scrap of paper, 'I sEnd yoU thiS in ToKen oF The WorD yoU pLedGed mE iVAn PETrovicH.' Didst thou not also plight *me* troth, Ivanusha my beloved?"

She paused and sat smiling, her eyes aglow with remembrance. "What happened then?" I asked. "Did he marry you, or was he angry?" "Oh yes," she said, "he married me, and yes, indeed, he was angry. He married me the next day, and the next night took me away in a freight car, alone next night in a freight car, alone at last with my lover. And he beat me sorely for giving the money to my father, but it was his right and I knew that he loved me and was my husband. I bore his first child in that freight car and my screams were matched by the cries of wounded men. One died with a moan as the child left my body. This here is our seventh, brave and strong like his father: you saw how he yelled and kicked against my breast." She patted the sleeping babe and closed her eyes.

Leningrad's Lucky House

LENINGRAD once had a Lucky House. Through its story flows the stream of life in modern Russia. Beneath new laws and customs lie old things unchanged. Even an ancient fairy tale is there — the Golden Fish.

In Leningrad in '22 — they called it Petrograd then, before Lenin's death — there was a dingy little house on the outskirts of the city. In it lived thirty-seven "souls," as the Russians say. Since the landlords had gone, the adults were grouped in a tenants' cooperative, according to Soviet rule.

They did not know how to manage very well, and got into debt. It was only fifteen rubles, but that was a big sum in those days for the poor. By an urgent and thorough canvass they raised twenty-five rubles, and for the first time had a surplus. In pride the cooperative voted to buy a ten-ruble ticket in the new state lottery loan.

One chance against millions. But miracles happen in Russian fairy tales, and their ticket drew first prize — a hundred thousand rubles.

Fifty thousand dollars in real money for a tiny tenement. The whole city, indeed all Russia, was excited. Memory of the black "hunger years" and currency inflation was still sharp, and real money was a novelty. Every man, woman and child of the thirty-seven souls was interviewed and photographed and paragraphed and broadcasted.

In its first enthusiasm the association donated ten per cent of the prize to the fund for homeless children. They then set to thinking how to spend the rest.

36

Leningrad's Lucky House

At once, it seems, the cares of wealth began. Nearly all Russian city dwellers are only a generation or two away from the country, and the ten adult members of the cooperative found themselves with more kinsfolk than they knew they had. Every living relative, up to cousins of the twelfth degree, wrote letters of affection, or hurried to the city bearing gifts, in the hope of sharing the golden flood. The money had not yet been paid, but in the Lucky House there was babble and feasting as they talked over their plans.

The spinster school teacher on the third floor, who had lost her job when her school was closed by lack of pencils and paper and fuel, was greeted by a brother-in-law, all smiles. He came with a suggestion about a small flour mill which was lying idle in his village. It could be leased for ten years at a nominal rent, in return for five hundred rubles' worth of repairs.

The Georgian couple on the first floor, who had been dancers but now lived by an older profession still, although the lady's charms were fading, found a warm friend in an uncle from Tiflis, who brought two plump goatskins of Naperiouli, red and potent as Burgundy. In happier days the uncle had been a prince, according to the Georgian custom which conferred this rank upon any one who owned more than five cows or fifty goats.

He had his eye on a dance hall in the care-free capital of the Caucasus, where men are bold and wild, and women are wild and fair. He hinted that the technical knowledge of his niece and nephew, both as dancers and in later days, would be of very present value; and that the investment of a thousand rubles would bring them rich returns.

In their room was a lodger, Vasilli Petrovich, aged eighteen. Vasilli knew what he was going to do with his money. There was a girl in the factory where he worked — Vera, her name was — and if only they could have found a room they would have been married already. But rooms cost money. And, beyond that, Vera's people were old-fashioned. They wanted a proper wedding, in church, and

37

a feast afterwards. They could not believe that signing the Soviet Register was enough.

They had brought Vera up in the old-fashioned way, too. She had never sought adventure with boys, like so many girls today. Vasilli liked that really; because he wanted to get married for good, and have a home, and babies; as did Vera. But there was always this hard problem of finding a room, and buying furniture. Nor would the wedding and the feast cost a kopek less than forty rubles.

If Vera's father had not hurt his spine when he fell off a truck in the war, or if her mother had not been unwilling to leave him alone while she went out to work, perhaps Vera's ten rubles a week would have been her own to spend. She might have agreed to drop the feast and the priest, and just go and get registered, and pay only the small fee of fifteen kopeks for the stamp on the marriage certificate, and come and share Vasilli's narrow quarters in the tenement. But she had refused to leave her parents, and the boy had despaired. Now, of course, it was smooth sailing for both of them, and for her parents too.

The unskilled metal worker with his wife and four young children in the stuffy cellar decided at once upon three square meals a day for a month. Then they would buy some clothes, and squeaky, shiny, leather shoes — that sign and proof of success in the Russian village — and with them they would go back home to the country.

They could get from the village soviet an allotment of the land which was lying idle because it needed a few hundred rubles for drainage. Their brothers and sisters and cousins had longed for this land, and so had the metal worker himself; but the desperate pains of living on the soil had driven him to Petersburg to work fourteen hours a day in the factory. When they had drained the land it would be the richest in the village. The former *mir* had often talked about getting the work done, and once had even tried to raise funds for it from the *Barin*. But the Barin had had a bad season at Monte Carlo, and nothing ever came of it.

38

Leningrad's Lucky House

Now, with six souls in the family, they could get eighteen *dessiatins* (about forty-five acres), three apiece, as the law said. There would be fifteen dessiatins more if their five unmarried relatives would join them to help them work it. Already they saw themselves as kulaks (rich peasants), perhaps even with a slate roof on their house, asking the village priest to dinner after church on Sunday — and the priest eager to accept, so rich would be their fare.

Upstairs, in a passage corner no bigger than a dog kennel, was Marfa Sergeyevna with her three young children, one already doomed with tuberculosis. There was hope for the other two, the doctor had said, if they could go to a sanitarium in the Crimea. But Marfa belonged to no Union, and the reference signed by her late mistress saying that she had served seven faithful years as scullery maid in the big house on the English Quay was no recommendation in Soviet eyes; nor yet that her dead husband had won the Cross of St. George to hold back some brief while longer the German troops from Warsaw.

But now Ivanusha would breathe the soft salt air, and watch the sea rippling blue, and the dark straight cypresses, and the feathery palm trees, to soothe his dying. And the two little ones would live and get strong — the doctor had promised it — once they reached the Crim.

So it was that each one in the Lucky House had a dearest hope, of love or comfort or greed or health.

And then, alas, the foul snake of Capitalism crept into the idyll. A discussion arose, at first mild but growing in acerbity, between two groups of tenants. How, exactly, should the money be divided? The party of the first part, henceforth known as the Capitalists, contended that the division of the prize should be in proportion to the floor space occupied by each member of the tenants' association, irrespective of the number of his dependents. On that basis, the Capitalist argued, they paid their rent.

39

Leningrad's Lucky House

The party of the second part, henceforth known as the Proletarians, claimed that the proper course was to divide the prize equally amongst all; that even the smallest babe was, *ipso facto*, a tenant, and therefore had the same right to a full share as anybody else. The discussion became a dispute, the dispute a crisis. Finally they went to law.

The People's Court settled the case in short order. "Whereas: the prize was won by the tenants' association as such, composed, as the record shows, of ten members, here as follows enumerated . . . the Court decides that the prize shall be divided among said members according to the area of floor for which they pay rent; that is, in proportion to their stake in the aforesaid tenants' association, irrespective of their progeny or dependents."

What joy in the ranks of the Capitalists! What bitterness in the Proletarian camp! Nine thousand rubles for the Georgian couple. That would start two dance halls in Tiflis. But for the metal worker and his wife and their brood of babes, only a thousand rubles by this rule of floor space. How would that drain the farm, and buy seed and plows and horses, and cows and pigs and poultry, and the solid slate-roofed house?

And what of Marfa and the dying boy who shared her mattress in the angle of the passage, and the two smaller children slung in their basket overhead? Passages are not counted in the calculation of Russian floor space. Marfa paid no rent, and was, in fact — in fact and in law — no more than a courtesy member of the tenants' association. The Communist judge had dealt justly according to his lights, but his verdict stole life and hope from the fatherless and the widow.

Only Vasilli did not care. As sub-tenant of the Georgians, he would receive for his corner of their room, which was the largest in the house, fully three thousand rubles, perhaps more. Vera and he had found an apartment, with two clean light rooms, sharing kitchen and actually a bath with only three other people. It cost three hundred rubles to secure "title" — against the law, of course, but everyone did it. Allow two hundred more for furniture, and for the church wedding and the feast say another hundred — why, if Vasilli got a thousand he'd have more than enough.

But up in her attic the spinster teacher Maria Nikolaievna brooded. The long draughty room, the bare uneven boards were transmuted by this verdict into gold. A full member of the tenants' association, she occupied — it was there in the record — not less than a quarter of the floor space of the whole tenement. Her share was therefore twenty-two thousand five hundred rubles, exactly.

Her brother-in-law had embraced her when he heard the court's decision, and his fat daughter had danced gurgling around them.

"Not one mill, but three!" he cried. He had had a notion of two others, but that, he thought, would require Capital. He breathed the word with reverence. And lo! Maria Nikolaievna was become a Capitalist.

Now, in her attic, Maria Nikolaievna brooded. At the far end of the room the brother-in-law snored, dreaming of mills. On a pile of coats his fat child whimpered in its sleep. "Stomach-ache," thought Maria resentfully. Greedy pigs, both of them. Never had she seen a child stuff itself like that! The same fat cheeks and beady eyes as its father. Not a trace of her poor sister. What claim had they on her anyway? Never a word or a line until now. What good would it do her to get twenty-two thousand rubles if it was only to go to these strangers? And that Georgian woman, how she had gloated when the verdict came. . . . Nasty creature, with her oily husband. . . .

Gradually, subconsciously almost, she came to a decision. The money must be distributed equally among all the tenants, young and old. The verdict must be upset. . . . The Proletarians had found a champion.

Beginning with no clear motive, Maria Nikolaievna soon found herself aflame with the passion of a Joan of Arc. Her eager speech rallied the Proletarians to new effort. From factories and clubs she

41

collected petitions. She besieged offices and anterooms, importunate as the widow of Scripture.

At last a retrial was ordered.

The Appeal Court, packed with workers, heard the whole case from the beginning, probing every detail. Then came the verdict, wise as Solomon's in its neglect of Law's letter for the spirit of Justice.

"Whereas: the verdict of the People's Court," read the presiding judge, "was based upon a narrow interpretation of the law determining the status of tenants' associations, and neglected to take into due consideration the basic principle of Soviet jurisprudence, namely, that the interests of the poor and humble shall be protected, said verdict is declared null and void. The Court of Appeal holds it important that in this case of universal interest there should be demonstrated the equality of all Soviet citizens, irrespective of sex or age. Furthermore, it is undesirable to permit discriminations of an economic or financial character to operate to the detriment of the weaker members of this communal group. The Court therefore decides that the prize shall be distributed equally among the thirty-seven souls domiciled in this building."

The Proletarians had triumphed! Maria Nikolaievna was a heroine — to all save her brother-in-law.

But, as the Bolsheviks have learnt, the demon of Capitalism is not so lightly exorcised. After the first shock of dismay, the adversaries rallied. The uncle from Tiflis had a compatriot, high-placed in the Commissariat of Justice in Moscow. Let them, he said, take the case to the Supreme Court there, away from the atmosphere of popular agitation which had influenced the Appeal Court of Petrograd, and all would be well. What was more, he added, the decision of the Supreme Court would be final. If they won in Moscow, that would end it; there could be no reversal.

And so at last the case came before the five judges of the Supreme Court of the Soviet Union. No vociferous witnesses here, no eager public, no impassioned words. Quietly, at leisure, the judges pondered the facts and coldly shattered all the glittering dreams.

Both the lower courts, the verdict stated, had failed to remark the essential feature of the case, namely, the status of the tenants' association as an Entity or Legal Personage. The title to the money was vested in the association, and the funds must therefore be devoted uniquely to the purposes for which the association existed, that is, to the maintenance of the premises concerned and to hygienic and cultural measures for the welfare of the tenants.

Thus Leningrad's Lucky House might shine with tiled bathrooms and polished plumbing, might blaze with electric lights and gayly painted walls; there could be a reading room with a bust of Lenin in eternal bronze, and instead of the dirty courtyard a garden pleasance ennobled by a marble Marx. But not one single solitary kopek might anyone, single or married, adult or child, put into his individual pocket or spend for his own ends.

Is not this the story of the Golden Fish, which every Russian knows?

A poor fisherman lived with his wife in a hovel by the sea. One day he caught a fairy fish, who promised to gratify his desires in return for life. The fisherman went home and told his wife of their good fortune. She wished for a stone cottage, a cow and a horse, poultry, and a pig. The fisherman went back to the shore and called aloud upon the fish, whose golden head emerged at once from the waves. The wish was granted.

But the woman's appetite grew with eating. Soon she sent her husband to demand a fine house, with plate glass windows and powdered flunkeys. Again the fish performed the miracle.

Again the wife became dissatisfied. She rose by rapid stages from rich bourgeoise to noble, from noble to tsar, from tsar to that distant figure whose medieval fame reached darkest Russia, the Pope of Rome, with power to bend the proudest monarchs of Chris-

43

tendom to his will. Here was the final miracle; the fat peasant woman a-seat in St. Peter's chair, with the papal tiara on her brow.

But over the Pope there is One Master. Drunk with ambition she craved divinity. For the last time the golden head of the fairy fish gleamed among the waves.

"Back to your hovel!" he cried, and vanished.

And the couple ended where they first began.

44

The Spirit Within

PHILIP PUTNAM pulled himself up to a sitting position with his back against the wall. As he did so his right hand touched the ground and pain ran like fire along his arm. The wrist was already swollen double, and he could feel the grinding of the broken bones below his thumb.

He bit his lips and the faintness receded. Thank God, the women had gone, Dr. Nelson's wife and her niece, who ran the dispensary. Nelson was right after all and he was wrong. Putnam had said, "It is our duty as missionaries to meet them without fear. Let us carry on as if nothing were happening. They are men like ourselves; why should any of us run from danger?"

But Nelson knew better. "Not this Blue Dwarf outfit," he said. "They are devils, this crowd. Of course you and I will stay, but the women go this morning on the Tupan's boat, and at that if I hadn't saved the life of his Number Two wife we couldn't get a place for them. I tell you, boy, this Blue Dwarf's bad medicine. If I had my way you and I would go too. A change of generals is nothing in China — I've seen scores of them — but when half the city runs away, as they are doing now, that means trouble. But you're in charge here, and if you stay I stay with you. But — you don't know the Blue Dwarf."

Poor Nelson, killed wantonly on the Mission veranda. Putnam shuddered as he could hear again the dull thud of the spear when it met the doctor's chest and the grunt of the soldier who drove it home, and the gasping whisper as he bent over the dying man, "Goodby — I'm lucky — it's quick. Oh, Lucy —"

45

The Spirit Within

Then a rush and swirl of yellow hands clutching and the stinking cloth around his mouth. He had struck back, despite his will to suffer meekly, fighting against suffocation — to get air into his lungs. He never felt the blow that broke his wrist, as he lost consciousness. And now here he was in the darkness, waiting — for what? He fumbled for the lighter in the inner pocket of his tunic, spun the wheel and looked round him by the glow of the little flame.

He found himself in a low circular room about fifteen feet in diameter. There was no window, and the floor, ceiling and walls were of stone. Near the broad wooden door, which was reinforced with iron scrollwork, was a row of shelves. On the floor beyond the door another man lay motionless. Putnam pulled himself to his feet and staggered toward the shelves, holding the lighter aloft. Yes, he was right; it was an oil lamp beside the earthenware bowl. Resting his wounded arm on the shelf, he clumsily lit the wick. The lamp was full; there would be light for several hours. The bowl beside it contained water. He drank greedily and bathed his forehead. The man on the floor groaned.

Putnam dipped his handkerchief in the water and knelt down to help his fellow prisoner, then started back, and the wet linen fell from his hand. It was the Bolshevik Shurof, whose bribes and propaganda had robbed the Mission church of half its converts and lured away two-thirds of the older pupils from the Mission school. Shurof, the enemy.

Kneeling, Putnam prayed for guidance, and there came to him the words, "Love your enemies and do good to them that hate you." As he bent again over the Russian and wiped his forehead with the dripping handkerchief he deliberately put his weight on his injured hand with a pain so sharp that he could hardly keep from screaming. How dare he judge a fellow man!

Shurof opened his eyes, staring blankly like a young child that has not learned to focus. He raised himself on his elbow and muttered some words in Russian.

46

"It's all right," said Putnam in English. "Wait a minute; I'll get you a drink," and brought him the bowl.

Shurof drank and smiled. "That's good," he said in Chinese, the only common language between them. "Well, comrade, those bandits have made a nice mess of us, haven't they?

"I killed seven of them before they got me; then some big ape swung a pole as I was slipping a new charge into my gun. *Chort*, how my head aches!" He passed his hand across the right side of his forehead where there was a broad blue bruise, then he pulled himself up to a sitting position and looked at Putnam. "I suppose you have no kind of weapon," he said, "and that damned lamp has no glass or we might use that. Perhaps if we broke this bowl and got a sharp edge it might do the trick."

"What do you mean?" said Putnam.

"Happy dispatch. I suppose you know that it's the Blue Dwarf who's caught us, and if you haven't heard what he does to prisoners, I have; in fact, I saw one or two — afterward — on my way here from Sinkiang. *Not nai-iss*," he drawled in English.

Putnam felt cold at the back of his neck. That was what Nelson had meant, "I'm lucky — to die quick." Despite himself he moistened his dry lips with his tongue.

"He likes it, that blue-faced rat. Why in the name of hell didn't the gunpowder kill him instead of spotting his face all blue and green? Sadic they call it — he gets pleasure watching torture. My father told me of one of the Whites like that up in Mongolia — Ungarn something his name was — a crazy Baltic baron, who killed all Red prisoners as slowly as he could."

His voice rose on the last words, and Putnam put out his right hand in a soothing gesture, then grimaced at the sudden pain. "You are hurt?" said the Russian. "Here, let me look at that. I'm no doctor but they make us take a first-aid course before they send us out on jobs like this. Did you?"

"Oh, no. We always have a medical assistant in our missions, but they killed him."

"Lucky devil! Anyway, let me look at your hand. Oh, yes, simple fracture. Where's that handkerchief, and have you anything hard that might help to hold it in place?"

"This lighter and my fountain pen."

"That'll do. Wait a minute; this will hurt a bit; I've got to pull on it. There, that's over. Now hold the pen there while I put the other thing here and tie it up with the bandage. I know it hurts, but you'll feel better afterward."

"Thanks," gasped Putnam.

The Russian jumped to his feet and stretched himself. Putnam's mind flashed back to a Harvard-Yale game when he had taken a message from his mother to a cousin who wore the crimson jersey. The boy had been knocked out and carried off the field. When Putnam reached him in the dressing room he had recovered from the shock and was standing in the same attitude as this Russian now, with his hands behind his head, stretching out his chest as the tide of strength flooded back into his veins and muscles.

He felt a sudden contempt for his own narrow shoulders and skinny legs and said abruptly, "Didn't your Communist — er — converts help you either?"

Shurof shouted with laughter, "Damn it, no; mine ran away too. Rice Christians, they call yours, but I'll tell you, comrade, mine were rice Communists also. *Chort*, if I'd had six of our Kursanti boys I'd have chased this Blue Dwarf back to his mountains. But no, they're soft, these Chinese — no backbone."

"Did you know he was coming?" asked Putnam. "The Blue Dwarf, I mean?"

"Of course I knew — ah, you're asking why I didn't run away. Well, you see, I'm Red Army, really, and the Red Army doesn't

48

run away — can't let these people think we're scared." He rubbed his chin with his thumb. "I had no definite orders but I suppose I *ought* to have taken cover. The movement was going nicely and we might have worked underground to take advantage of the confusion caused by the Blue Dwarf's attack. You see," he added naïvely, "I've not had much experience at organizing work. I left the military academy only three months ago. But why did you stay?"

"I had to," said Putnam slowly. "My orders were quite definite."

"Do you mean to say," cried Shurof, "that your people expect you to wait for certain death? Why, it's nothing short of —"

"Not my people but my Chief. He did it Himself, you know."

"I don't understand. No sane man would expect —"

"My Chief is not a man. He is God."

The Russian stared at him, wide-eyed. "You don't actually believe that stuff?"

"Of course I believe it; that's why I'm here now. Why do you think I came to Sechuan in the first place if it was not to obey Christ's orders, His definite orders to teach His gospel throughout the world?"

The Russian grinned boyishly. "I thought that missions were part of your capitalist system, just a form of political and economic penetration. They are, too, and you can't deny it — or maybe you needed a job. I've heard there were ten million unemployed —"

"I wasn't unemployed," Putnam interrupted. "Besides I have money of my own. I came to Sechuan because I felt it was my duty. I was warned of the dangers, but that is nothing. I too am a soldier, in a greater army than yours."

The ring of conviction in Putnam's voice affected his companion, but the Russian's eyes were still incredulous. "You surely know," he persisted, "that religion in any form is simply one of the means by which the chains of class tyranny are riveted upon the masses, that it is reaction of the most subtle and dangerous kind. Why, in the U. S. S. R. the priests always opposed —"

"I don't know the U. S. S. R., but you are wrong about America. My faith is not reactionary and its first principle is the absolute equality before God of all mankind."

"But the Church is a *part* of capitalism, one of its strongest pillars. Everyone knows that. What does your church do for people in America or anywhere except frighten them with hell-fire and spend in charity a tiny fraction of the money exploited from the workers? Does the church cure unempl —"

"It preaches love and brotherhood instead of strife and class hatred like your Bolshevism. What has Bolshevism done for you, when it comes to that?"

Shurof's eyes flashed. "For me, everything," he said simply. "My father was born in a filthy cellar in Petersburg. He was the only one of seven children who lived to manhood. At seven years of age he was working twelve hours a day in a bottle factory — of course, no education — but somehow he managed to live. I was born in an attic, high up under a tin roof, stifling hot in summer, and in winter the snow came in through the cracks. The revolution gave me everything, and my father too. He joined the army, learned to read and write and fight against oppression. He was decorated for courage. He became a man instead of a slave. My mother died of pneumonia that first winter of '17, when I was only three. They put me in a children's home, gave me the food and air and sun and education without which children wilt and perish. They sent me to school and trained my mind and body, taught me games and discipline and collective action, and finally I was sent to the military academy as one of the Kursanti — officers' training corps, you would say — to learn to defend the people's cause and our socialist fatherland against capitalist aggression. That's what Bolshevism did for me, as it is doing and will do for countless millions. Now tell

50

me what your church has done for you. How did *you* live as a boy, and your father before you?"

Putnam was slow to answer. He thought of the pleasant house near Boston: built by his great-grandfather with its Early American furniture and shady lawns; he thought of Groton and Harvard and the smooth sheltered safeness of it all. How could he explain that to this Russian? But he had to try. When he had finished, Shurof said wonderingly, "But all you are saying is that America and your ancestors gave you what you've got; that capitalism gave it to you; that, thanks to your ancestors, you became a member of the privileged class. You're not capable of understanding how the masses live and feel."

"I'm not," said Putnam hotly. "I worked four years in one of the poorest parishes —"

"Never mind that. The thing is that your consciousness has been formed by your environment, like that of everyone else, and you owe that environment to your country and your family, not to the Church. What has the Church done for you, for you yourself? I'm not asking now what it does to the American masses, because I know the answer to that. But don't you see there is nothing in what you have told me about the Church doing anything for you. You are the product of your class, your privileged class. What part did the Church play in your development as Bolshevism has played in mine?"

Putnam stared at him in dismay. Honesty compelled him to recognize that there was truth in Shurof's words.

The Russian pressed his advantage. "Your Christianity has done nothing for you whatsoever save to give you ideas, or ideals if you like, which in your case may be genuine but nearly always are hypocritical and have no sure foundation in fact or logic. It's a dream, your Christianity: you can't *prove* a thing about it, whereas our cause is real."

Still Putnam was silent. He was exhausted and his arm ached

51

horribly. He could not escape the parallel between Christianity as a belief and Bolshevism as a belief, nor refuse to admit how much the latter had done for Russians like this man beside him and how little Christianity was responsible for the life he himself had led. He felt that somewhere there was a flaw in Shurof's reasoning, but he did not seem able to find it.

Suddenly light came to him; of course there was an answer. "It is strange," he said, "that you Bolsheviks, who lay such stress on planning, cannot see that the whole universe moves according to plan and not by accident. We must assume that there is a plan and purpose, which in the final issue is what we Christians mean by God. We believe that He has chosen to communicate a part of his purpose to humanity, that there is a spark of His life in our bodies which distinguishes men from beasts and that that spark will never die. Take us now here, the two of us, for this is the final question: What have you to look forward to after tomorrow? At the best no more than sleep."

The Russian nodded. "I shall probably be glad of it by the time they've done with us," he said with a shiver.

Putnam refused to be checked. Now, he felt, he was on safer ground. "At last," he said, "we have reached the real crux of the matter. You can argue and make a strong case of it that Bolshevism has done more for you in life than Christianity has done for me, or for my people at home. In life, yes, perhaps, but that is the least of it, because death is not the end."

"Death *is* the end," said the Russian.

"Well, I know it isn't, and that is why I am happier than you are at present. You are stronger than I am and probably braver. You may die in silence while I am forced to scream. Yet what does that mean? To you it means that everything you've lived for and worked for and are ready to fight for just ends blankly with the slamming of a door, but to me death is not the end but the gate to life eternal.

For you a hole in the ground; for me the great reward, the glory of my heart's desire. I die joyful."

This time Shurof was silent. He looked earnestly into Putnam's shining eyes. "Do you really think that?" he asked.

"I know it. In this hour there are no more bars between us, you and me. Both of us in our different ways with different backgrounds have dedicated our minds and bodies to a life of service, to an ideal outside ourselves. For you too, therefore, there is hope, if only you will listen — and believe."

Shurof shrugged his shoulders. "No, no, comrade, that's no good. You can't catch me with your 'opium for the people' — although opium has its uses; I wish I had some right here now." He paused a moment and continued unexpectedly, "It does seem stupid somehow to finish like a candle that's blown out. I had so much to do, there is so much to do, and I have done so little. Damn it, I'd like to think that somehow I could start again, not in your heaven; I don't care about that, but here on earth. I am not afraid to die, but —"

Without sound or warning the door swung open, and there stood a thickset man not more than five feet tall. He wore a gray silk robe buttoned up to his throat; his hairless face and bald head were thickly pitted with blue-green powder marks. Behind him two guards carried torches, huge men in khaki uniform with broad-bladed executioners' swords across their shoulders, each hung on a blue cord with blue tassels. There was a blue arm band on the left sleeve of their tunics.

"I am Wu-Ming-Fu," he said smoothly, "better known to you foreigners as the Blue Dwarf. No, no, young man, keep still," as the Russian braced himself for a spring. "You are young and strong but my guards could break you with one hand. Don't move, I tell you; it pleases me to talk with you." His voice was light and soft but his eyes were hard and cruel as he watched them. He came forward and

53

one of the guards reached back for a tall gilt chair upon which the
little man sat with his soldiers standing beside him.

While he sat there in silence two other men came into the room,
dragging a big unwieldy object of metal which looked like a lathe
for machining tools. Its upper surface seemed browned as if by
rust, and Putnam eyed it blankly, but the Russian had once seen
the Blue Dwarf's victims — afterward — and knew this instrument
of torture for what it was. He knew it so acutely that he could smell
the dry, bitter sourness of the clotted blood. Now he was looking
at the face of death's worst agony, but there was no terror in his
eyes.

For a long minute Wu-Ming-Fu gazed at his prisoners in silence,
then turned to Putnam. "Why did you come to China?"

"To preach the gospel of Christ."

"To Chinese heathens, you would like to add, who were civilized
two thousand years before your ancestors got rid of their blue paint
— have you never heard of Confucius? For what other reason did
you come to China?"

"For no other reason, neither for money, trade nor politics. I
came because I thought it my duty."

"Very good. And you?" He looked at the Russian. "Why did you
come here?"

"To teach slaves to fight for freedom," said Shurof boldly. "To
rescue the Chinese masses from their oppressors, native and foreign."

"And enroll them under the Red flag?"

"Yes," said Shurof, "the Red flag — of freedom."

"Administered by the OGPU as in Russia? You can keep that
kind of freedom. Tell me now, both of you, did anyone ask you to
come to China, any Chinese, I mean? No — you come with your
White Christ and your Red freedom to a country that needs neither,
that has been set in its own ways for more than four thousand years,

54

and you find — me. Now what do you expect from me?" He looked at Putnam.

"Death," said the American, and the Russian nodded assent.

"Are you afraid of death?"

"Yes," said Putnam, "I am afraid, but I am not reluctant."

The Blue Dwarf looked at his lathe of torture, then his eyebrows raised and the men beside it moved back. "I believe you," he said to Putnam, "young fool that you are, I can see a hope for death behind your eyes. What a sorry land America must be that its sons seek death so far away from home! Now what has the Bolshevik to say?"

Shurof waited, then spoke slowly: "I am not afraid, but I am most reluctant. There is so much for me to do and I have done so little."

Wu-Ming-Fu smacked his hand upon his leg. "That is good," he said. "The extremes which meet. One seeks death but fears to die; the other dies but does not fear. That sounds good and true to me. It is young and naïve but it is true, and truth, my young friends, counts more than your White religion or Red freedom. With this truth you have bought your lives.

"Take that away," he said. "I do not need it here," and the two attendants dragged the creaking metal structure away from the little room. He grinned at them and his eyelids twitched but there was no mirth or pity in his eyes. "I don't like foreigners," he said, "who come like a plague of locusts to devour my country. I had thought to make an example of you two, to leave you there for the others to see when I go from this city in the morning, not dead, perhaps, but in such a state that the greatest mercy would be bullets for you both. You deserve it, you damned foreigners whom no one asked to come here. But no" — again he smacked his hand upon his knee — "you have entertained me with your childish answers. That is fortunate for you. Wait here until tomorrow, because my men are wild and savage — they too hate foreigners. Then your

55

friends will come back. They will be surprised to find you both alive." He made a sign to the guards, who picked up the gilt chair and carried it away. The door clanged and the two looked at each other.

For a moment neither could speak; the change from despair to hope, from death to life, was too sharp and sudden. Putnam's whole body was shaking. He tried to control himself but the strain upon his nerves was overgreat. Shurof laughed harshly. "This time it is *I* who win. That devil has robbed you of death and snatched away your martyr's crown. But to me he gave back life and the work I want to do."

Putnam looked at him. "We *both* win," he said, "because we both have work to do."

The Thrifty Peasant
and the Precious Mattress

IN THE EARLY DAYS of Soviet Russia money was in chaos. Besides the official currency of the Soviet Republic, there were scores of others issued by local Reds and Whites and little mushroom states. Early in 1923 Soviet banknotes were replaced by a new ruble equal to one million rubles of money issued before 1921. The next year still another ruble, a "gold" ruble, was made equal to fifty thousand of the issue of 1923. So it came to pass that fifty billion of the old rubles were needed to buy one of the new gold rubles. This, perhaps, Ivan Ivanich Popoff never understood.

Ivan Ivanich was a pillar of society in the village of Arkangelskoi, fifteen miles from Moscow. After he had done his duty in the Polish War he went home to the village, to his wife and three children and the little truck farm. Not many months later the coming of the N.E.P. (New Economic Policy) gave hope to the Russian countryside, which had grown weary under the food levies of the period of militant communism. Now those days were past. The new slogans were "Hard Work and Economic Prosperity," "Peasants Produce Food for Payment," and "The Link between Peasants and Workers is the Keystone of the Revolution."

Ivan Ivanich was a hard worker, and so was his wife Anna. Even the children were old enough to have learned their father's habit of labor. He knew the modern ways of farming, too. He had been a prisoner in Germany and had been sent to work on a farm near Hirschberg in the rich Silesian Valley. There he had learned what could be done with poultry and cows and vegetables, for the city

57

markets. Let the other peasants raise hay if they wished, and plant rye and oats. He knew better, so near the gates of Moscow. Peas and beans and pumpkins and lettuce and fat summer asparagus on the sandy strip where nothing else would flourish — that would pay best on a five-acre farm. Chickens and ducklings that the twelve-year-old girl would care for while the boys helped their father, and Anna bought milk and skimmed it to make cheese and butter and fed the pigs with the swill.

Anna's brother had a stall on the big Smolénsk market in Moscow. He was a stupid, greedy fellow — though honest with his relatives — who loved display. He changed food for jewels, so that his wife wore rings on her fingers and a thin plantinum and diamond bracelet round her fat red wrist.

But Ivan Ivanich knew better than to waste money on such playthings. In Germany he had learned to figure and to keep accounts. Every Sunday night, when he came back from market with his bag of paper money, he put all the items down in a notebook, costs and receipts, sales and profits. Each Sunday showed business bigger and better, by thousands and thousands of rubles. His gains were fabulous.

Always he followed the same routine, sitting hunched over the table writing big round pencilled figures in the book beside the lamp. The children watched him, quiet as mice, while he wrote and added and subtracted. This, too, was hard work. "There is a devil in the book," he used to say when the totals would not tally, a trouble which came often. The smaller boy, who was only six, did not dare to touch the notebook except in the daytime and when his mother was in the room.

But at last the figuring would be finished and Ivan Ivanich left with the pile of bills which showed the week's gains, thousands and thousands of rubles. Each Sunday the profits were bigger than the week before.

Then he would get to his feet with a sigh of relief and call

58

The Thrifty Peasant and the Precious Mattress

"Volya" in his deep voice. The older boy, already on tiptoe, would run forward, throwing a look of contempt on his sister Katya as he passed her. Girls knew nothing about money; of course they were left out of a weighty business like this.

The father crumpled the money into a ball in his strong fist, and then, slowly, let it fall into his son's outstretched hand. Volya held it a minute, proud and smiling, then bounded to his parents' bed and burrowed in the mattress.

The mattress was the pride of the Popoff family. When Ivan Ivanich came back from the war, rich in knowledge of accounts and truck farms but poor in goods and threadbare after his imprisonment in Germany, the mattress worked on him like balm. How Anna got it, in that night of loot and arson when the village raided the farm and stables and mansion of their absent lord, she never remembered. But there it was in her cottage next morning, a noble foreign mattress, stuffed with horse-hair, soft and spacious. And there were woollen blankets, light as thistledown, warm as the sun of summer.

"This was all I got," she told him, pretending to be humble, "this and some of the prize poultry. Those stupid fools wanted to kill them, but I saved two roosters and twenty hens. The children and I have slept well and warm these winters. No peasants in Russia, Ivanushka, have a bed like ours."

She spoke true. Ivan knew that after the first night in his own house. Already he was rested and refreshed, after the twelve nights on the floor of a box car.

Often the neighbors said to him, "A smart woman, your Anna. Do silver cups make tea sweeter, or has soup a better flavor from a painted bowl? But all of us, peasant and lord, spend eight hours of the twenty-four in bed. 'A sound sleeper makes a good reaper,' as the old people say. . . . Yes, she's got sense, your Anna. You're a lucky man.

So each Sunday night the boy Volya ran and burrowed in the

mattress, and scuffed out a handful of horsehair, and put in its place the crinkly ball of bills.

Katya had done it once, because it was her birthday, that first Sunday when Ivan Ivanich came home with profits from the sale of eggs and slim spring beans which would have startled his German master. And she was the eldest, two years older than Volya, and so it was her right.

But the second Sunday she was betrayed by feminine vanity. Instead of putting the money into the mattress quickly, she stopped. Then she asked, "But, Daddy, couldn't we take some of it to buy shoes for me and Mother and the boys?"

They were too surprised, all of them, to answer. Katya stood in the middle of the room, feeling suddenly lonely. Her face went red and tears began to roll down her cheeks. Without another word she gave the ball of money to Volya — it was only a little ball then — and threw herself upon her mother's lap and sobbed.

Anna's kind hand patted her daughter's shoulder, but there was nothing to be said. They loved Katya as much as before, but always after that it was Volya who performed the weekly ritual; except on the last Sunday in the month, when Sasha, the younger boy, was allowed to do it. No one ever said anything to Katya about what she had done, but always when the moment came, on Sunday night, Volya and little Sasha gave their sister the look which said, "Girls do not understand about money." Katya always felt ashamed.

The summer of '22 was a golden harvest for Ivan Ivanich. There were big restaurants open now in Moscow; and cabarets where new rich Nepmen drank and feasted all night, as in the old days; and gambling rooms where the green tables were covered with Tsarist ten-ruble gold pieces and foreign banknotes. And the foreign missions, and the four big houses for the Americans who brought food for the Volga famine, helped to swell the demand for eggs and poultry, butter and vegetables and cheese.

Ivan Ivanich bought a horse and cart, and no longer carried his

60

stuff to market in sacks and baskets. He made three journeys a week instead of one. His wife's youngest brother, who did not have to serve his time with the army because he had only one eye, came with his wife to help them. She was a strong fair girl from the north, who had no equal in fattening a goose.

There was no room for them in Popoff's cottage, but a neighbor gave them lodging with board at a fair price. The Sunday night ceremony went on as before, but now Volya must burrow two or three times in the mattress, pulling out hair in handfuls to make room for the ball of bills.

The fat geese at Michelmas fetched rubles by tens of thousands, and the turkeys for Christmas tens and tens of thousands more. Ivan Ivanich could scarcely believe his eyes as he pored over the figures. Again and again he added, subtracted, and gazed wondering at the total. There it was in black and white, beyond a doubt. He was rich, enormously rich; richer than his old lord had been; richer no doubt than any man in the world had ever been except the Tsar.

The mattress was stuffed with his wealth. It was less comfortable, perhaps, than it had been, but Ivan and Anna slept each night on a rosy cloud of dreams.

They had heard much of America these last months, that marvelous land beyond the seas where even the peasants ate meat every day, and magic rooms of steel leapt upward to the tops of giant buildings in the time it took a dog to scratch a flea.

Of course there were scoffers who doubted these marvels, but were not these Americans spreading food across Russia as a man scattered grain in the spring? And had not one of them paid Ivan Ivanich himself a hundred thousand rubles for a turkey, and laughed as he took the bird away?

Ivan had been at first ashamed when it happened, but later a friend showed him a picture of the chief city of the Americans with its towers that stabbed the sky. Under the picture were strange let-

61

ters printed. Ivan Ivanich could read quite well, but these letters puzzled him.

His friend smiled. "I thought you would not know," he said. "They are so rich, those Americans, that they can afford to write in their own way."

"So do the Germans," said Ivan doubtfully.

"I spit from the roof upon the Germans," said his friend. "Let me tell you the meaning of these American words."

Following each letter with slow finger he read out, "New York, city of millionaires and millions," and looked at Ivan in triumph.

Ivan Ivanich accepted the new faith. He thought often of America, flowing with millionaires and their millions. There he would go to join them, and live in a high tower with a magic cage of steel, and be great amongst the great and happy all his life.

He told no one of his thought, not even his wife. But he cherished it, as he sat waiting for bed after supper, and fondled it again more dearly in his dreams.

One sunny February morning, when the air was full of the flecks of light that come with the coldest frost, Moise Abramovich Rabinof came to see him. The Jew was known to Ivan Ivanich because he had tried to buy for a good price a jewel from Ivan's brother-in-law. But the brother-in-law was foolish, and he kept the jewel.

The visitor accepted a glass of tea and began a long talk about high food prices and the great profits that citizen Popoff must be making. Citizen Popoff let him speak, knowing well that the real purpose of his visit would be shown later.

Step by step Moise Abramovich moved on to the comfort, nay, the luxury, of the Popoff home. For Ivan Ivanich this was too much. He answered that neither he nor his wife ever wasted a kopeck on such folly.

Did the fellow want to sell him something, he wondered. If so, he would have his journey for nothing.

62

The Thrifty Peasant and the Precious Mattress

The next words explained matters.

"Is that so, citizen?" purred the voice. "I had heard that you lived here like a lord, and slept in a lordly bed, a big and beautiful bed, soft and rich."

Ivan's face brightened. Here was a famous joke, to fool the clever Jew.

"Not a bed but a mattress," he said modestly. Then he added with emphasis, "A soft mattress indeed, and rich. Yes, rich and precious; oh most highly precious."

Moise Abramovich settled himself in his chair. He had been correctly informed. The Americans would pay him fifty dollars — a hundred gold rubles — for a good horsehair mattress. To clean it and buy a new cover for it would cost two or three rubles. If he could get it under seventy it would be good business.

"I am ready to buy your mattress," he said, "and for a good price. You know that I offered your brother-in-law a fine sum for that ring with the brilliants."

Ivan Ivanich chuckled inside himself, but no smile showed on his face as he bent forward to haggle. What a splendid joke! He would spin it out a little longer, to see the Jew's face when he learned what the mattress was really worth.

"In all the world," he said, "there is no mattress like this. I cannot sell it. I cannot even set a price upon it."

Moise Abramovich frowned. The peasant watched him with a crafty smile.

"There is nothing without price," the Jew said at last. "Listen, my good Ivan Ivanich. You shall fix the sum yourself and I will pay you."

Ivan Ivanich drew a deep breath. Now he would spring his joke.

"Very well," he said, "as you are a friend of mine, I will tell you the price of my mattress. But I warn you it is not cheap."

"How much?"

"You can have it as it lies for three hundred million rubles."

The Thrifty Peasant and the Precious Mattress

His guest calculated. Three hundred millions . . . that meant sixty rubles at the current exchange.

"All right," he said, "I accept."

If a thunderbolt had struck Ivan Ivanich he would not have been more surprised.

"What! You accept . . . three hundred million rubles!"

"Of course," said Moise Abramovich.

"Three hundred million rubles!"

"Let me look at this mattress of yours," said Moise Abramovich. "If I am satisfied I will give you the money at once."

He felt of the mattress and punched it. He seemed puzzled. "I thought it was a horse-hair mattress," he said. "This feels like paper."

In a flash Ivan Ivanich realized that the Jew knew nothing. He had only been pretending. He had no idea of the true value of the mattress.

"Look a little closer, my friend," he said, "and perhaps you will understand. Look at the paper you speak of. You will see that it is a very precious mattress."

The Jew's face cleared as he examined the crumpled bills of all denominations from hundreds of rubles to tens of millions.

"Yes," he said, "I understand. This is where you keep your savings. All your savings, yes, for the last three or four years. How much is the great total of it all?"

Ivan Ivanich hesitated. Was it wise to tell? . . . But why not?

"Three hundred million rubles," he shouted. "Not one of you tricky Yids was ever so rich; nor any mattress so precious."

Moise Abramovich was stung by the term of scorn.

"You are wrong!" he snapped. "There was once a mattress far more precious than this."

"Where?" asked Ivan Ivanich. "When? How?"

"Right here, four years ago." An ancient hate flared in his black

64

eyes. "For this mattress stuffed with horsehair I would have given you four hundred millions. See! I have it here in cash."

He showed a packet of bills with figures higher than any Ivan Ivanich had ever seen.

"See what you have gained by your years of work and saving, you poor fool! We tricky Yids at least know the difference between gold and printed paper. Each new bill they print drains value from those before it. Today I would give you eighty rubles of gold for your mattress of horsehair, but I would give you only sixty rubles for your heap of paper. Tomorrow I will not give you so much for your pile of paper — fifty gold rubles perhaps. And next week less — twenty. . . ."

A fist hard with work crashed against his teeth. Roaring with anger the peasant fell upon his visitor. He beat him without mercy and threw him from the door.

"Begone from here, you Child of the Devil, before I kill you!" he bellowed. "Cheat! Robber! *Boorjui* (bourgeois)! Blight on our Russian land!"

The Jew picked himself up and fled.

Soviet Justice hears all races, all creeds. Three weeks later the People's Court gave trial to the plea of Moise Abramovich Rabinof for damages to salve assault by Ivan Ivanich Popoff.

The Court had trouble in making the matter clear to the defendant, who made a poor impression. One of the assistant judges later called him a regular *kulak*, the worst type of grasping peasant.

On the other hand, as the presiding judge remarked, the plaintiff's injuries were slight. He seemed to have been more frightened than hurt.

Citizen Popoff was required to pay citizen Rabinof damages to the extent of five gold rubles — two hundred and fifty million rubles paper at that day's rate of exchange — and to pay one gold ruble costs. That was three hundred millions paper in all. Proceedings showed citizen Popoff to be in possession of just that amount. The bills were seized by the court.

Whereupon citizen Popoff, who had acquired fresh savings of several tens of millions in the last three weeks, went forth and spent them all on bootleg vodka. He was carried home at midnight to his cottage and put to sleep on the mattress, stuffed with hay.

Under Sentence

AMERICAN REPORTERS in Moscow get letters every week from people asking if Russia is safe to live in, and can they bring their wives and, if they get a job, will they always have enough to eat? And what about disease and, anyway, is it *safe?* It's hard to answer the letters because we don't know their wives, or whether they would like the job when they get it, or whether they think of "enough to eat" in terms of caviar and steak or black bread and cabbage soup.

But we do know Russia's safe, at least relatively safe; that the Civil War is over and there's no shooting in the streets, and no more epidemics, and nothing especially wrong except that you can't get rich. There's never been a pauperocracy before but the Bolsheviks have made one, where the poor are safe. Take the case of Barney McGubbin; he found safety in Russia, and a job and a wife, and enough to eat. And he found safety from federal justice and from private vengeance, and safety from the thought of the Chair and hell's fire after. Oh, yes, Russia was safe for Barney and he played safe when he went there: he said he did; he knew he did, "the safest thing I ever done," he said. "I thought I was sunk," he said, "till I saw that advertisement, and then I played a hunch and, believe me, I played *safe.*"

We were thumping back from Leningrad in the fastest train in Russia; sixty miles an hour in places, which is mighty fast for Russia; sixty miles an hour they run her, which is much too fast for Russia, where roadbeds are not good and rails are not good, and maybe some bolts are missing, and a freight train ahead has stalled

67

Under Sentence

her engine maybe, and no one noticed it. Until the express crashes her and the fire blazes up and the injured begin to yell, and pray for you to shoot them before the flame grills them. They have a lot of train wrecks in Russia. Russia is safe but Russian trains are hazardous, and I don't like train wrecks; I've had only one but it was one too many and cost me a foot and seven months' pain and various operations. I don't like pain and I don't like being vivisected, so I wasn't buoyant that evening in the train from Leningrad when I met this Barney McGubbin.

Not until I saw his wife, I wasn't, but she took my thoughts off train wrecks, and off what would happen when we hit the rail where the bolts were missing. If Saint Anthony had seen her she'd have taken his thoughts off his Bible. . . . Wasn't he the one whom devils tempted in the shape of women? . . . But she wasn't like that; in her there was no devil: gay and friendly like a child no one's ever been harsh to, with a little wise smile and eyes full of sympathy, and a blue beret to match them and a honey frock to match her hair. That was Nora Petrovna, the loveliest thing I ever saw, all alone at a table in the dining-car of the bounding train.

So I sat down and forgot my nerves and we began to talk. Her voice was like rippling water in summer and the chime of bells. She spoke of her husband by his name in Western fashion, Barney McGubbin; spoke with love and pride, how strong he was and brave and what a worker. The Red Banner they gave him, she said, for valor in the war days, and the Order of Lenin for building a blast furnace at Makeyeva. And now, she said, they were going to Kuznetz on a structural steel job.

"There are delays," she said, "the program lags, they need men like Barney. He will drive them with shouting to twice and three times' effort, and they will not mind because he drives himself and does the work of four. I am glad that you will meet him and write of him in your newspaper for all to read, for Americans and Russians

68

too, and our comrades in other countries, as a model for them to follow, to come here and fight for Socialism, to fight and build the Workers' State and the future of the world. I shall read what you write with pride; it is a great and splendid story, the story of the fighting and building of my husband, Barney McGubbin."

Poor child, she did not guess that story as I write it now.

Then Barney came to join us, a big man with black eyes and a high color, and a jovial Irish burr in his voice. He wore high boots and leather breeches and a khaki tunic, and the two red badges for work and valor were pinned above his heart. We dined and drank wine and talked, but Barney said no to vodka. "I've got better," he said, "than that, but we'll drink it later, when the girl's asleep. She says it tastes like medicine, poor darlin'; she's the sweetest creature in the wurrld, but never a one of these Russians can ever appreciate whisky."

Nora Petrovna went to bed — we sat on talking, and Barney loosened his tongue and told me of his life.

As a young man he was rough and tough, it seems, and defiant of authority, and he joined the I. W. W. back in '16 for fun and the sake of a fight. "'Wobblies,' they called us," he said, "and them was wild days in Colorado, with strikes and rushing the scabs and battles with mine-guards and state police. Say, man, it was good while it lasted, but they were too strong for us, and some of us skipped to Seattle and raised trouble there. Then there was a dock strike at Oakland, and they got me there with a bunch of the boys and framed us . . . three years in San Quentin prison.

"When I came out in '20 the Workers' cause was all shot, the boys were dead or jailed or jumped their bail and gone to Russia, but prohibition was just beginnin' to flourish. So I get me into the bootleg game, Detroit to Windsor across the river, and that's where I shoot this federal cop and get in bad.

"But I fooled them," Barney boasted; "yes, I fooled them when

69

they thought they'd got me. There was one, ye understand, who was worse on me than all the rest, a bitter devil he was, by the name of Red Gordon; he was after me like a hound on a hare. He was buddies, it seems, with this guy I shot, they was buddies in the war. And he'd swore he'd get me if he combed red hell to find me, and sit me in the Chair." His eyes quivered round the edges like an animal's when the knife's at its throat and it feels death coming. He took a big drink of whisky, shook himself, and went on with his tale.

"I was lying-up in Hoboken . . . the room was on the third floor, looking over the street . . . a gurrl I knew, she took me in . . . wouldn't sell me for any reward, nor care what I had done, you know the way some of them are.

"And one evening, about six it was, I see this Gordon, see him plain under the lamp. I tell you, man, he was sniffing for me like a terrier dog at a rat hole, sniffing the air for me scent he was, like he knew I was somewhere near.

"'Ellen,' I said, 'there's Red Gordon, down right there under the lamp. And I'm a dead man,' I said, 'and may Christ have mercy on me soul, for He knows I'll need it, me that'll burn in hell for ever and ever.' I was scared plumb through, ye understand, with the strain and all, there was no heart in me.

"'Don't be a fool,' she says. 'If he knew where you was he'd 'a' come straight up the stairs with his gun at you. He may be sniffing your trail,' she says, 'but he ain't found it yet, however close he is, and you come out now with me, down the fire-escape at the back of the hall, into the little alleyway at the back; it's dark there and he won't see us, and we can slip round to the room of a friend of mine; she's away but I get letters there and she leaves the key for me under the mat. Come on now, Barney, they ain't gotcha yet.'

"I'd never 'a' done it alone with that fear in me bones. . . . I was soft and shaking. When we stood in the dark alleyway I darsn't move, but she dragged me along. 'Come on,' she says, 'pull yer hat down low and square yer shoulders. It's only a step round the corner, and we'll fool the sniffing hound and tangle his trail for him. He shan't have you tonight, I tell you, and tomorrow's another day.

"So we got away clear. The house where her friend lived, ye understand, it was one of these houses where they ask no questions, and in the morning she slipped out to buy some food and saw no sign of Red Gordon. He didn't know her anyway, but she'd seen him in the lamplight, and there was no sign or trace of him.

"I felt better then, and shamed for the fear that was on me, and I ate no breakfast and read the morning paper, and there I saw this advertisement I was telling ye of. 'MEN WANTED,' it said, 'Skilled Workers Needed for Soviet Russia. A Party Will Sail This Week Direct for Petrograd. No Scabs or Yellow-bellies Need Apply,' and it gave an address where to write.

"I wrote and told them the truth, some of it. I told them I'd been a Wobbly and how the police framed us in Oakland and we went to jail, and how they were after me again with another frame-up and would they help me get to Russia where me comrades were, and I gave the names of some of them. But didn't tell them me own name; I told them the name of one of the boys who was with me in San Quentin; he'd gone up in the woods in Oregon, and I guessed they wouldn't know him; that was the chance I had to take. I sent the gurrl with the letter and about noon she came back and said it was okay. . . ."

The Polish war had ended when Barney arrived in Moscow, wearing his own name again and warmly greeted by old comrades. He joined the League of Political Prisoners, which has great prestige in Moscow, and those who knew of his murder of the police officer accepted easily his word that the crime was political. "Political killing is not murder," Lenin had written, and so deep was the hatred for "gendarmes" in Bolshevik hearts that the "liquidation"

71

of a policeman was meed of praise, not blame. That autumn he enlisted in the Red Army and won his decoration at Perekop, the last and bloodiest battle of the Civil War, which opened the Crimea for the Soviet advance to throw Wrangel, the last of the "White" generals, into the sea.

"They sent me next to lower Asia," he told me, "where Enver, the Turkish fox, had thought to build him a new empire. Cunning as a fox he was, but he fought like a wounded tiger when we trapped him in the mountain pass where he'd holed up.

"That was a good fight, that was, and I took a lance-point in me arm and the lad who held it got me saber through his neck. I was singin' to meself by that time, 'Hallelujah, I'm a BUM, Hallelujah, I'm a BUM,' with a cut for each BUM, and all of a sudden it was finished, and Enver was dead, and after that there was no more talk of empires in Soviet Asia."

So Barney went back to Moscow a war hero, with wound and medal and the rank of captain, and had the time of his life, he said. The city was wide open then in the second year of NEP . . . cabarets and girls and dancing and plenty of food and liquor. But he was a member of the Communist Party by this time, and soon he was appointed inspector on the railroad between Moscow and Kazan, to see what kept the trains from running on time and to make them run on time, or anyway to make them run.

"And all me previous experience of railroads was six weeks as a pick and shovel man on the New York Central," said Barney, grinning, "but they do things like that in Russia. You know how they are yerself. And I took it gladly, I was weary of playing the fool. There's something about this country that gets you, you want to join in the drive of it and do something with the rest of them. Lord knows there's enough to do.

"Down there in Kazan station, my second trip it was, I got the shock of me life. Me train was just pulling out and I sat at ease in a private compartment when another train come in across the plat-

72

form and there in a doorway stood Red Gordon, as plain as I see you now. I ducked like the snap of a knife and me stomach felt sick. I'd the fear of him deep in me bones, ye understand, it was stronger than me. I had to fight meself to me feet to reach up and look out of the window, but he hadn't seen me. I watched him get off quite slow and careless and walk the other way as we left the station behind.

"That was a bad night for Barney, you bet it was, and the month that followed. There were hundreds of Americans in Russia then, doing this relief work for the famine, and a good job they made of it, but never a one of them named Gordon, and I could get no check on him. But I knew — oh, yes, I knew — Red Gordon wasn't feeding babies, he was trailing me, sniffing along on me trail till he found me and paid me for what I done to his buddy. And I was scared he'd get me, scared right down inside me. Just think of the nerve of it, him a foreigner after me like that in Russia, where he was an enemy and all of them my friends. But I couldn't check on him nohow, and that scared me too. I began to think I was going crazy, and me friends took notice.

"'What's wrong with you, Barney?" they said. 'You look sick and you're nervous. You're working too hard,' they said, 'you need to rest up a bit, there's no call to kill yourself with work.'

"Aye, them was the words — 'kill yourself' — and I often thought of it, thought that was the best way out. And then I saw him again, and this time he saw me. We'd slowed down at a place where the line was newly double-tracked, going not more than ten miles an hour, and another train passed us the opposite way, going slow as us. I sat by the window, and as the other train passed I saw Red Gordon sitting by the window, and *he* saw *me*. Our eyes met and his face lit up like a window in a dark house when someone puts the light on, and he smiled and nodded, very sure of himself, the way a man smiles and nods when he sees an old friend. But his

73

eyes weren't friendly, no, his eyes were *not* friendly, not to *me* they weren't, not at all friendly but sorta *satisfied*."

The whisky bottle was empty and Barney McGubbin grabbed his bag and pulled out another and broke the neck against the table and poured out half a glass and drank it quickly. The restaurant car was chilly and he wore no coat but there were beads of sweat on his cheeks and forehead. He licked his lips and sat silent, eyes staring.

"Yes," I said, "and then what?"

He gave a quick shake of the head, like a man that wakes suddenly from a doze. "Have some more," he said, "this is good stuff, none of your Russian vodka; this is real Irish whisky, I got it off an Irish captain in the port last night. And I'll take some more meself and drink to that same Red Gordon. He loved his buddy, and me he hated, but I loved Russia, and Russia killed him for me. That same night he saw me I came to a junction some hours later, and the first thing they told me was the train we'd passed had gone through a bridge down the line and the wrecking crew was ready and would I go along.

"I went and I slept all the way, without fears or dreams. I knew it was ended somehow, either him or me. I'd hardly slept for weeks, but that night I slept well. It was light when we got there and some peasants were helping to get out the injured and there was a lot of noise and yelling. But Red Gordon didn't yell; he lay quiet with a broken neck. He was smiling his satisfied smile but his eyes were shut.

"That was ten years ago, ye understand, and I've married the sweetest gurrl in the wurrld, and worked hard, and they think a lot of me. I've no more fear of Red Gordon, or the Hot Seat, or the fires of hell to come after. I've no more fear at all. . . . I'm sure and free and *safe* in Russia."

Then we went to bed and I wondered how much of it was true.

74

A reporter can't believe everything he hears, and not always everything he sees. But I thought Barney McGubbin had told the truth, and I thought he was mighty lucky, with a wife like Nora Petrovna, and *safe* in Russia, safe from Red Gordon's vengeance and the electric chair and the fear of hell fire. That's what I thought until one day three months later I met an American specialist who'd worked at Kuznetz, and asked him if he knew Barney, "a big fellow, black Irish," I said, "with a beautiful Russian wife; he used to belong to the I. W. W. and is now a Communist."

"Yes," said the engineer, "I knew him, and if I'd not played baseball in the old days I'd be with him now."

"Where's that?" I said. "And why baseball?"

"I dunno where," he said; "I'm not religious. . . . But I'm not with him because baseball teaches you to move quick. I'll tell you about it, if you like.

"I've been in steel ever since I left school, and it's a tough business, and I've put up steel all over the world, and I thought I'd seen all of it. But this Kuznetz baby, she was something else again. Mud . . . Lord, man, she was ten feet deep in mud, and in the summer it was dust, and in the winter snow and ice, forty below zero. You've got to hand it to these Russkis, they have nerve. To build the biggest steel plant in Europe, or Asia, 'cause it's Asia really, way beyond the Urals, out there on the steppe, miles and miles from anywhere. The plans were all right, *we* took care of that, but getting the stuff there . . . one line of railroad. . . . Oh, boy!

"And building a town at the same time, and getting food . . . I don't know how they stood it. We got *our* houses built, they gave us the best they had, I'll say that for them, but tough . . . Gee, how tough it was. And that mud. You see *they* did the town planning; *we* were only responsible for the plant, and they got the elevation wrong, or forgot to build any roads. They had a few tractors, but you couldn't use autos or trucks, just horses and wagons, and if they got stuck you took a gang with ropes and hauled them out.

75

Under Sentence

I'd like to see some of the boys at home build blast furnaces on those terms . . . that'd show them what raising steel meant.

"We were putting up Furnace Number 2 when this Barney Mc-Gubbin blew in, and believe me, I was glad to see him. I'd lost twenty pounds on Number 1. The skipbridge slipped when they were raising her and squashed a dozen of them the way you squash a fly. . . . Oh, we had a hell of a time . . . but Number 2 was worse. You see, they'd learnt something about it by then, and what the risks were, and they didn't like it. I thought it was bad before, when they took chances with Number 1 that turned my hair gray, but at least they weren't scared . . . not till that skip fell . . . but *that* kinda worried them. It's bad enough to work with a reckless crew, but perfect ruddy hell with a crew that's scared.

"I don't care if Barney was ten I. W. W.'s, I wouldn't have cared if he'd been a murderer, the way he made them work and made them *like* it. And work himself. . . . Gee, I tell you, boy, that man did the work of five. *And* the way he drove 'em! . . . I thought I knew something about driving men, but he drove 'em and made 'em like it. You see, he was quite a big Communist and had been in the army — they said he was a general or something — and had a raft of medals, and he talked Russian like a streak. He used to sing to them, army songs in a big, deep voice — he had a swell voice — came over to our place sometimes on rest days and sang that Wobbly song, 'Hallelujah, I'm a bum,' till the plaster fell off the ceiling. So they forgot about being scared and worked like beavers. When he came we were way behind on our schedule with Number 2, and in a month we'd 'caught up and surpassed it,' as the Russkis say, and were sitting pretty. We raised 2's skip without a hitch and believe me, I was glad when *that* job was over. I'd not been out of my boots for forty-eight hours (we had to wear high boots on account of the blasted mud, high rubber boots) nor Barney either, but when the skip was up I went to bed and slept sixteen hours.

76

"The next day was rest day, and Barney came round and brought his wife. . . . You're right, she was a pippin, and crazy about him, and we had a real party, in honor of Number 2. You see, we'd broken the record for construction speed and beaten Magnitogorsk right off the map, and the Russian chief was there and mighty affable and complimentary to me, but he knew and I knew that Barney deserved the credit. And when they were going away Barney's wife said, 'Mister,' — they all of them called me Mister 'cause they couldn't pronounce my name — 'Mister,' she said, 'your rubber boots need patching and so do Barney's. I've found a man who can do it, so let me take yours with his. They'll be ready in two days, and if you don't they'll just go into holes. It's better to have wet feet for a couple of days than for all the rest of the spring.' So I let her take them, and if I'd not played baseball and learned to move quick . . . well, I'd be with Barney now, wherever that is.

"There were three teams next morning with a load of castings, two horses and two men to each team, and having a hell of a time. They were stuck in a pool of liquid mud like pea-soup, up to the knees, and the horses were slipping and plunging and the drivers were shouting and cursing, and altogether it was as fine a mess as you'd find in Russia, which is saying a lot. I was going along to Number 2, along a railroad embankment just above 'em, so I must needs slide down and try to help. But they couldn't understand me, or didn't want to, and I might as well have kept my feet dry, when along comes Barney, from the other direction, and he took charge and began to talk to them in Russian they *could* understand, telling 'em what to do. 'All of you push the first wagon,' he told 'em, 'and get her out, and then go back and push the next; that's the way to do it.' And he lined 'em up, and me too, and pushed himself, and the horses pulled, and she began to move.
"Right then while we're all pushing, there appears from nowhere a casual Russki *tovarish* with a coil of wire over his arm, stringing a

77

phone line or something, plashing through the mud without a care in the world. He's got to get this line strung across the town, but just above us, a couple of yards or so from the embankment, there's an overhead cable, so he halts and gets all set to throw his wire over it. Which cable is a naked power line carrying fifty thousand volts.

"I was busy pushing and didn't notice, but Barney did, saw him swinging his arm all ready to throw the wire over the cable. '*Look out*,' he yelled, 'that's a *live wire*, you'll. . . .' But he spoke in *English*, can you blame him?

"I told you I'd played baseball, and I moved *quick*. I just dove for that embankment like it was first base, and I reached it. I pitched on my head and turned a half somersault and saw what happened.

"The Russki comrade threw his wire, a big coil of it, and it went over the cable and rested on the cable, and the end of it fell down on the wagon. The full force of the current hit them like lightning. The horses went up in the air on their hind legs and fell in heaps and never kicked. The tovarish catapulted backwards and lay still. The other men jerked all ways, you'd have thought there were springs in them. Barney kept his feet, but his arms shot up as if he was praying or addressing a crowd, and his face went blue. He stood there what seemed a long time, then suddenly fell forward in the mud. I used to think electrocution was merciful, compared to hanging, and it sure is quick; but, my friend, what a ghastly death!"

The Woman Who Could Not Sleep

IN AN Ukrainian village there lived a prosperous couple who seemed to have no troubles in life, but were burdened by a secret sorrow. They had no children.

The husband, Danchenko, had been a rich peasant before the war, owner of eighty acres, two mills, six cows, and four fine horses. At the time of the Revolution he was a man about forty, thick-bodied and strong as Ukrainians are, with dark hair, high color, and bright passionate eyes. His wife, Maria Petrovna, was swarthy and tall, "a horse of a woman," as they say in the Ukraine, who could do a man's work in the fields.

Danchenko put his whole heart into the land. He was popular in the village, though that did not save his land or cattle in the great upheaval. But he won the gratitude of a Red Army division by warning them about a White attack. He had no cause to love the Whites, Danchenko. They had looted his grain, taken two horses, and killed two cows he was unable to conceal.

The Red Commander was himself of peasant origin. He stayed at Danchenko's farm, and admired it. In '22, as president of the provincial soviet, this man was called upon to select managers for the model Soviet farms into which a part of the estates of former landlords had been made. For once he ignored the usual policy of giving such posts to Communists.

"Danchenko," he said, "is a farmer, with real feeling for the land. We have too many talkers already. What I want is some one to teach the peasants how to get results."

As manager of the model farm Danchenko was in his element. A

79

thousand acres instead of eighty, tractors instead of horses, fairly abundant capital and labor — what did it matter to him that the land was not his own? After all, he had no sons, to take it when he was dead.

His wife, too, was happy. No more drudgery in the fields, but managing dairy and piggery, poultry and new fruit preserving plant, with lectures for the peasant women. Now, like her husband, she had little to regret from the Revolution.

But in their hearts there was still the common sorrow. They had no children.

So they adopted a boy — there was no lack of orphans in those days — a strong healthy lad of thirteen or fourteen, named Alexander. Sasha, as they called him, quickly made friends, and in six months it seemed to Danchenko and his wife that the boy had been with them always and was indeed their son.

A year passed, and then a shadow darkened their lives. Maria Petrovna began to love Sasha not as a mother but as a woman. She fought against it at first, and tried to hide it. But as the months went by and the boy became more manly her passion carried her away. Soon all the village knew. Danchenko alone refused to believe it. . . . The thing was unnatural, impossible.

But one warm summer evening he could doubt no longer.

For him the position was appalling. His horrified outburst beat impotent against Maria's will. Shameless, she told her husband that she loved Sasha and must have him. It was wicked and dreadful, he said. To her that did not matter; nothing mattered, save Sasha. Twenty years of marriage, reputation, self-respect — they were nothing to her.

"It is like a fire in my heart," she cried, "which burns and burns. I must have him. You cannot stop me. It is not his fault — you know that. But you shall not stop me."

The man walked out through his familiar fields. The breast-high

80

wheat gleamed silver in the moonlight. He twitched an ear from its stalk, husking the grains between finger and thumb.

"It's ripe," he muttered. "We must cut tomorrow." A moment longer he stood, then turned and walked back to the house.

The next morning, without a word to his wife, he sent Sasha to stay with a friend who ran a flour mill at the other end of the province.

Maria was beside herself. She would get a divorce at once, she said, and go after the boy, to be near him. She was a woman possessed. For hours she stormed at her husband to know where Sasha was gone. She ran through the village asking, careless of what they thought. Once she rushed off to the orphanage where Sasha had been. A fortnight later she came back, pale and beaten.

At first the village women smirked and whispered. She took no notice and the gossip died. To her husband she was like a stranger in his house. Then, little by little, she came back to him, until by Easter he believed she was healed of her madness, though its memory remained a barrier between them.

On Easter Sunday Danchenko, as manager of the model farm, gave a feast to all his workers and some people from the village. They stuffed themselves with food and drank strong beer and vodka. Later on they grew noisy, and told coarse stories, and shouted with laughter.

Danchenko was arguing seed-grain with the president of the village soviet when suddenly there was a stir at the other end of the table. His wife Maria had sprung to her feet, white-faced, furious, her finger pointing at a man two places down.

"You filthy svoloch!" she cried. "Get out of here! Get out! How dare you speak to me of that!"

Her voice was low, but so harsh with pain that the company was frozen into silence. A woman near Danchenko crossed herself hurriedly. Maria seemed fighting for further speech. Her lips moved and the muscles of her throat quivered. She made a gesture towards the door, and the man arose and shuffled out.

She stood for a moment watching, then turned and ran out of the door leading to the house.

There was some more talk and drinking, and a half-hearted attempt at the songs that should have kept them merry late into the night. By midnight the last had gone, with muttered excuse or furtive sympathy.

Danchenko sat down at the table, chin resting on clenched fists. From time to time he poured a glass of vodka. The fiery spirit was tasteless in his mouth. This was the end. He had stood too much. The Ukrainian stubbornness which until now had forced him on to work and live his life as usual heated slowly into rage. He crushed his glass upon the table and felt no pain as the fragments cut his hand. Then he went upstairs.

His wife was huddled in a far corner of the room, swaying her body and moaning, with the boy's round cap held tight to her breast. He saw she had his big revolver in her lap. Torn pieces of the bedspread were scattered across the floor.

As he moved forward, she jumped up and ran to him, holding out the gun. "Take it — You! And kill me! I can't do it. I meant to, but I can't. You must kill me, now! I cannot bear it."

"What do you mean?" said Danchenko. "Are you mad?"

She threw herself at him in a frenzy, clutched his hand, twisted his fingers round the pistol. "Sergey — do it! You must do it!"

In anger he fought her back. "O Christ! I've stood this long enough. . . ."

And the gun crashed twice.

She lumped against him, and he coughed as the smoke filled his nose. She pulled herself upright, panting. "Oh. . . . I feel . . ."

She choked; smiled; whispered, "Thank you, Sergey," and fell dead against the wall.

His rage burnt out, he wrapped the body in the bloodstained rug and carried it downstairs. The first thin streak of dawn was showing in the April sky, but no one stirred about the house. They were sleeping off the Easter feast.

He put his bundle on a wagon, harnessed the horse, and chose a broad flat spade. He drove along the rough track to a field fresh-turned for the spring potatoes. There he buried her, without anxiety and without haste.

To his plain peasant mind, this was not his wife he had killed, but a tortured spirit he had set free.

The farm was still quiet when he came back to stable the horse and wagon, carefully rubbing out the tracks. He went upstairs, cleaned the revolver and locked it up, and washed away the last traces of blood. He packed some of his wife's clothes in a bag and hid them in a cupboard. Then he lay down upon the bed and slept.

It was noon before he came into the big living-room where the farm workers were waiting for their midday meal. No one seemed surprised when Danchenko told them his wife had left him. She had been very angry, he said, the night before, and had gone away. He did not wish to talk of it, and they would all understand. Perhaps she would come back again. They all knew the story. He need not speak of it any more.

He sat down at the head of the table and began to joke with a red-cheeked girl about her lover, just as he used to do.

He really felt that a weight had gone from his shoulders. The workers on the farm noticed it, and the people in the village. They spoke of it little, except to say that Danchenko seemed gayer, more like his old self. He was absorbed once more in willing service to the land.

The rhythm of peasant life flowed on. The calves were born, and the little pigs and ducklings. The fields were planted and the grain was sown, and a live green carpet covered the earth in the magic of a Russian spring.

May passed, and June. The spring crop stood knee-high, and the tall winter wheat was yellowing to harvest. In the potato-patch near the farm white flowers had begun to gleam through the thick foliage that hid the murdered woman lying three feet below. She was, it seemed, forgotten.

But as the days lengthened, Danchenko grew troubled. It was not remorse, or even regret; but something deeper. An ancient fear came back to gnaw him, the old belief that the dead who lie in ground unconsecrated can never rest at peace; but must rise each night to wander unseen and sleepless till the Judgment Day.

All rancor had left him, and there was no scar of crime upon his heart. He had begun to think of his wife as if she had died a natural death, quite long ago, before the blight of incest and despair.

It was not the terror of a ghost to drive him, but sheer swelling pity for the lonely spirit that must stray forever above the common fields not marked by God for man's last resting-place.

The thought of her wandering soul became too powerful at the last to be withstood. One night, in the short hour of darkness between twilight and dawn, he rose and took the cart and dug the body from the ground. He worked in a wild rush unlike his former care. He left a shocking hole in the potato patch, and a bloodstained kerchief and a matted braid of hair.

The wheel tracks led straight from that hole to the village churchyard. And there in a corner they found next morning a fresh-dug grave. He had not even put the cart back into the barn. On it were signs that none could miss, and the rank odor of corruption.

It hung about him too, as he lay full-dressed on his bed, with muddy boots, when they came to arrest him. He was sleeping heavily, and seemed dazed when they woke him. But they did not think he had been drinking. He nodded when they charged him with the crime, and went with them without speaking — like a man in a dream — as they led him away to prison.

The Magic Egg

MAXWELL BLACK regarded his nephew severely. "I disap-
prove," he said, "of all these Russian ideas. They are . . . ah
. . . subversive and fundamentally wrong. Equality, for instance,
is admirable as an ideal, but in practice . . . preposterous. At your
age, Jim, I know Ideals have . . . ah . . . weight, but we older
men must deal with realities, with . . . ah . . . life as it is, not as
it *ought* to be. I do not wish to boast, but it was attention to facts,
not fancies, during the last four years that has enabled me to show
you this interesting curio, Professor Dwight. There it is, exactly as I
told you, almost a perfect oval, except for the slight pointing at
this end; in fact, as I said, a golden egg."

"Doesn't want to boast," thought Jim Black angrily; "the old
boy's as proud as a peacock. Just because he was cautious and
thought things were too high six years ago and sold out and bought
Liberty Bonds, does he think that makes him a successful banker?
And traveling round the world and collecting 'interesting curios'
. . . and people think he's a financial wizard and all, but he can't
fool me. He's just a golden egg himself, a pompous golden egg."

"Weigh it in your hand, Professor," his uncle continued. "Surely
it is too light to be solid, yet the most careful examination has
failed to reveal any . . . ah . . . aperture."

The professor took the curio, a shining yellow oval, exactly the
size and shape of a hen's egg but overlaid with tiny plates like the
scales of a fish, upon which a bewildering maze of lines had been
engraved, and fumbled excitedly for his glasses.

He fitted them on his nose and held the egg up to the lamp

above the dinner table. "Good heavens!" he cried, turning to his host. "You said you got it in Shanghai . . . Shanghai . . . that's impossible."

Maxwell Black was ruffled. "It came into my possession," he said, "precisely as I told you. I was walking along the Bund in Shanghai when this man accosted me . . . a native . . . although not very Chinese in appearance . . . rougher-looking . . . and . . . ah . . . more hairy. He just said, "Fifty dolla," and pressed it into my hand. He seemed in a state of urgency, and . . . ah . . . nervous tension, which somehow communicated itself to me. I acted with unaccustomed precipitation, gave the man fifty dollars, and he turned and ran, yes, sir, ran as if the devil were after him. Curiously enough, I had no fear that I'd been swindled, and when tests were applied I was not surprised to find it was indeed gold. I —"

"And that's all you know," the professor interrupted. "You didn't inquire, you haven't — ?"

"That's virtually all," said his host. "I left Shanghai the same evening, and put the egg in my suitcase and forgot all about it. After my return to New York I showed it to one of the assistant curators of the Metropolitan Museum, who thought it might be Tibetan in origin, but had little else to impart. And it was not until Lampson here mentioned that you were visiting his place in the country to rest and compile your account of your last expedition to Tibet that I thought of it again and decided to ask you — "

"Of course it's Tibetan, man," snapped the guest, "but do you know what it *is*? Why, this is *The Missing Egg*. . . . There were two, you know, laid by the Dove in Paradise . . . the Panchen Lama is supposed to have taken this one with him when he fled to China. The other is still in Lhasa. My friend, the Dalai Lama, showed it to me . . . even opened it and told me the secret, though of course he wouldn't let me touch it . . . there are *some* limits.

86

"Yes, yes, it is identical . . . now, let me see. . . . I follow the line, then press this scale . . . and this . . . yes, there's the curve again . . . and here . . . and here . . . and . . . *it opens*. You see . . . the scales cover and disguise the point of juncture . . . and here inside is the pip, the miraculous pip from Eve's apple." From one of the halves of the egg with trembling hands he shook out onto the tablecloth a dark object which did in truth resemble an apple pip, magnified ten-fold in size.

For nearly an hour the professor held forth about Tibet, its mysteries and customs. The pip, he said, was dark jade of great antiquity and was reputed to give the egg magical qualities. He replaced it carefully in its golden case. He did not know precisely what the magic was, the subject was too sacred. The Dalai Lama had said this and the Panchen Lama had done that, and so on in an endless monologue, which ended in stupefying Mr. Black and his nephew and the fourth guest, Black's partner, Miles Lampson.

As the professor paused at last to drink a glass of wine, the young man created a hurried diversion. "That's all most interesting," he said, "amazing in fact . . . and I envy you, Professor, to have spent so much time in that marvelous country. But," he continued firmly, as the professor showed signs of answering, "that does not affect what I was saying before, that the Russians are right in trying to abolish class distinctions in their new society."

For once Maxwell Black leaped eagerly to an argument about the Bolshevism he dested. "It's all so absurd," he said. "If you destroy initiative, what is left?"

"The collective farms will supply a different initiative," his nephew said. "Kulak individualism was antisocial."

"Nonsense," snapped his uncle, "you can't run a farm like a factory."

"But Russia isn't America, Uncle Max," Jim countered. "The

87

kulaks tried to hold back the clock of progress and got what they deserved."

The banker pointed the small end of the golden egg, which he had picked up from the table, right at his nephew as though it were a gun. "I tell you," he said, "no one can ever treat American farmers like that; they wouldn't stand for it. In fact, it seems to me these kulaks were a poor, spineless lot to allow — "

"They had no choice. Besides, public opinion was against them."

"I don't believe a word of it . . . to lie down meekly under such tyranny . . . no American would stand it. I wish I were a Russian kulak — "

Suddenly he was caught in a whirl and swirl of flashes and darkness, swift as lightning, terrible as thunder. Then the butt of a rifle struck him sharply between the shoulders as a voice bellowed, "Get on there, damn you."

He lurched against a telegraph pole and fell headlong into the dry ditch beyond. A hard hand jerked him to his feet, and he stood there aghast. Instead of his New York dining-room with its shaded lights he found himself on a gutted track winding through weed-choked grain fields. Beside him were two men, shoulders hunched forward as they slouched along. One had long, matted gray hair hanging below the collar of his black cassock. He wore a round black hat on his head and his face was bearded and damp with sweat. The other was a tall youth dressed in dirty patched calico. His blue eyes above beardless cheeks had the dumb misery of a steer that is being led to the slaughter.

A tall soldier in khaki, with rifle and long thin bayonet under his left arm, shook Black savagely, then thrust him forward. "Get on, you damned kulak," he shouted as he lowered the point of his bayonet, "unless you want a taste of this between the ribs."

In an instant of horror Black knew what had happened. The

88

golden egg was magical indeed, and the wish he had lightly uttered had been fulfilled. He had become a Russian kulak. The very language of the soldier was familiar . . . and worst of all, the egg itself had fallen from his hand when he lay sprawling in the ditch.

From the first he knew he was not dreaming. The pain in his back was real where the rifle butt had struck him, and the harsh rub of the canvas breeches on his naked flesh and the thick dark beard beneath a chin that had always been clean-shaven, and pungent dust that rose like smoke and made him sneeze. Yet there was no doubt of his own identity; his mind and memory were those of Maxwell Black. But his body had changed; the hard, lean form and swelling muscles of a Russian farmer had replaced the round paunch and heavy figure of an American banker of fifty. "I must see about that when I get back," he thought . . . "always meant to take more exercise. I'm hungry, damn it, and a highball would taste good in this infernal dust, but Max, my boy, you haven't felt so well since that last football. . . ."

When he got back! Good God, would he ever get back! He half turned with the wild thought of running off to find the egg . . . and saw the soldier close behind him with his long sharp bayonet sloped and ready. Escape was hopeless now, he must locate the spot. Right here was a milestone . . . one . . . two . . . three . . . yes, the third telegraph post beyond the milestone marked 9 — that was his goal. Again he looked back and caught the soldier's eye. What a malevolent brute the man was!

"Be careful, Maxim Maximovich," came a whisper from the young peasant beside him. "He's watching you. He'd stick you like a bird on a spit if you'd give him a chance."

His voice rose on the last words and the soldier heard him. "Shut up there — no talking!" he yelled.

The youngster cringed as if a whip had struck him and shuffled on

89

in silence. "Spineless," repeated Black to himself, but his own spine shivered from the near and ready steel.

The worst of it was that he hadn't the remotest idea of the reasons for his present plight — why he was under guard, what had happened and what would follow. His wish, it seemed, had been fulfilled literally . . . he had become a Russian kulak and therefore knew the Russian language . . . beyond that his mind was a blank. But he knew also that there was no chance of escape for the moment.

After marching a mile they passed through a wood and came out into a narrow lane on the outskirts of a small country town. No one took any notice of them as they turned a corner into what seemed the main street.

"Turn right," ordered the soldier, and they entered what was evidently the central square of the town, some fifty yards across. On the far side they came to a building in the style of a Greek temple with four massive columns, somewhat chipped and weather-beaten. The guard beat on the heavy oak door with the butt of his rifle. It was opened by a young man in black leather jacket and breeches, with a revolver strapped to his hip.

"I have brought the prisoners, Comrade," said the soldier, saluting him — "the priest Grusof, Timofei Timofeich; his nephew Konin, Ivan Petrovitch, and the kulak Chorny, Maxim Maximovich, all charged with murder."

The other gave the prisoners a cold, menacing stare.

"Quick, now," he said, "the court's waiting."

Black's first thought was that the place was more like the Baptist meeting house in the New England village where he was born than a court of justice. The guards, one in front and one behind, with fixed bayonets, led the prisoners to a pew-like bench on the right of a dais, where they were told to sit. Facing them in the body of the court were two or three hundred roughly dressed men and women.

90

Most of the women wore red kerchiefs and many of the men had a red rosette or arm band.

Immediately to their left was a red-draped table with three high empty chairs behind it and, beyond, another table also covered with red, where a short, stocky man in black leather coat and breeches was standing. He eyed them keenly as they sat down and made some notes on the pad in front of him. Black guessed that this was the prosecutor.

The soldier behind him barked an order so sharply that Black jumped, and all present rose to their feet as the judges entered the room. The leader was a squarely-built man of middle age with head and face clean-shaven. He wore military uniform devoid of insignia save for magenta lapels on his collar and the red badge of a decoration pinned over his heart. His eyes were cold and hard and his jaw long and cruel, but there was intelligence in the broad forehead, the height of which was accentuated by his shaven head. His two assistants were less notable. One, in rusty black broadcloth, looked like a workman in his Sunday suit. The other had the air of a young farmer dressed up for a county fair in clean white suit and trousers.

"I declare the session of the People's Court open," said the senior judge briefly, and everyone, including the prisoners, sat down.

The president whispered for a moment to the workman on his right, then rang a bell for silence. "We are awaiting witnesses," he said, "from the village of Masupovo, where the crime was committed. In the meantime I shall request the prosecutor to read the indictment."

He turned towards the prisoners. "Grusof, Timofei Timofeich, priest, aged forty-seven." The priest stood up.

"Konin, Ivan Petrovitch, farm worker, aged nineteen." The young man stood up. His face was white and his limbs trembled.

"Chorny, Maxim Maximovich, individual farmer and employer of labor, aged fifty." Black rose and looked firmly at the judge.

"I protest," he cried. "I am innocent."

91

The Magic Egg

There was a murmur of surprise among the spectators. The judge's bell shrilled loudly. "Silence," he cried. Then curtly to Black, "You will be heard later. Prisoners, sit down." He waved his hand to the prosecutor. "Read the indictment."

The prosecutor rose to his feet and, stepping out from behind the table, began to read from a long sheet of foolscap. The indictment, which evidently formed the whole case of the prosecution rather than a simple statement of the charge, declared that the two elder accused, Grusof and Chorny, had conspired to bring about the death of a school-teacher, Nadya Lvovna Lapteva, aged twenty-two, member of the Communist Youth organization since the age of seventeen, who had taken an active part in organizing the poor and middle peasants of the village of Masupovo in a Collective Farm. The crime had been committed at their instigation by Konin, the nephew of Grusof, an employee of Chorny. The victim's body had been found late at night three days before in a field formerly belonging to the accused, Chorny, which was now a part of the Collective Farm. Her skull had been smashed with inhuman ferocity and there were other bruises on her body.

Earlier that evening the younger accused, Konin, had been seen lurking by a clump of trees near the entrance to the field with a heavy sledge hammer which was the property of the accused Chorny. The said hammer was later found in Chorny's woodshed in a suspiciously clean condition as if it had recently been wiped.

The priest, Grusof, and the kulak, Chorny, had both contrived to be absent from the village the night the murder was committed, the former on the pretext of holding church services in a village twenty miles away, where he spent the night. The latter had chosen this occasion to come here to the county town, where he too had spent the night, for the purpose, as he declared, of protesting against a judgment of indemnity for injury to one of his employees. Nothing could be more significant than this coincidence of alibis. Further-

92

more, both the older prisoners had repeatedly, in front of witnesses, declared that Lapteva would come to a bad end if she continued to incite the peasants.

Other similar threats would be brought into evidence, the indictment continued. The motive of the crime was clearly established. The peasant, Chorny, had been the richest man in the village, a typical kulak who lived by the exploitation of his poorer fellows. The priest was the son of a kulak in a neighboring village and had acted according to kulak instincts aggravated by religious superstition. Finally, the prosecutor concluded, there was no one else in the village who would have dreamed of such a monstrous crime. Their murdered comrade, who had occupied the post of teacher for six months, was universally beloved. Her life was an example of Communist duty and devotion.

"The case," the prosecutor concluded, "is clear." He sat down amidst a hum of applause, which the judge allowed to continue unchecked. Then he turned to the prisoners. "Grusof," he said sharply. The priest stood up. "Tell the Court about your life and social origin."

In a quavering voice he related his life's history.

"Did you ever oppose the Revolution?" the judge interrupted.

"Never."

"Were you ever imprisoned?"

"No." And he went on to tell how he had lived during the past two years, "in peace and friendship with all men."

"But you spoke against the murdered girl since you came to the village?"

The priest was silent.

"Do you plead guilty or innocent of her murder?"

"Innocent. I swear by the Holy Book."

"Your Book has no weight in this court. Sit down."

The priest's nephew seemed so terrified that he was unable to speak audibly. After several attempts to make him talk the judge said, "I shall read the facts and you can shake your head or nod it to show whether you agree or not."

He stated the facts briefly with no sign of dissent; then it was Black's turn.

"Tell the Court when and where you were born and what was your social origin."

"I do not know," said Black firmly.

There was a murmur of surprise in the crowded room. Was this defiance or the simulated folly of a cunning kulak?

The judge's face hardened. "Sit down," he snapped. "I have met men like you before and dealt with them as they deserved." His voice was grim and his eyes were hard as steel.

"I now declare the Court adjourned for half an hour," the judge continued, "to await the coming of witnesses from the village of Masupovo."

When the trial was resumed it was clear that the prosecutor meant to waste no time in securing his verdict. Witness after witness testified to the threats uttered by the two elder prisoners against the dead girl, "whose noble efforts to rescue this village from the kulak grip and from outworn superstition," as the prosecutor put it, "had fanned to white heat the fires of anti-social vengeance." The motive for the murder was thus established.

Once or twice Black tried to defend himself or question details, but he was baffled by his own ignorance of the facts, and his efforts only drew upon him reproof from the judge. The priest's nephew, Konin, broke down utterly under cross-examination. Slobbering with fear, he was quite unable to explain why he had borrowed the sledge hammer.

Black intervened. "Was it to mend a fence or drive in posts?" he asked boldly.

"Silence," shouted the judge; and the prosecutor cried angrily, "How dare you put leading questions to the wretched instrument of your crime!" There was a savage growl from the audience, and the judge rang his bell repeatedly. "Prisoner Chorny, if you interrupt again, you will be gagged. Do you pretend now to remember on behalf of your accomplice, although during your own examination you played a complete loss of memory?"

"And after you had killed her, after beating her brutally to death," the prosecutor continued, "then, prisoner Konin, you wiped the hammer and took it back to the man who had given it to you and had given you your orders." The youth hid his face in his hands and stood there with shoulders heaving. "Answer me, at once," the command rang harsh and loud, "nod your head if you cannot speak."

To Black's agonized despair the tousled blond head bent twice in a definite gesture and the pent-up breath of the audience sighed forth like a distant groan.

"At last we get the truth," the prosecutor triumphed. "Prisoner Konin, sit down."

Black's brain was whirling as the last witness, a clean-cut youngster of twelve or thirteen in khaki uniform with a red tie, rose to explain how he had found the body late at night. The prosecutor let the boy tell his story without interruption. He was counting on the effect this artless recital of kulak revenge would create for his final speech. Black heard him dimly, without attention. If Konin hadn't killed the girl, who had? Wasn't there something he had read somewhere about a meteorite? . . . back home in America. The thought of his country roused him like a spur. He threw his head back, then bent forward to listen.

"And my auntie said, 'Aren't you afraid to cross the pasture next the churchyard after dark, Misha?' and I told her, 'That's a silly old story; we Red Pioneers know there is no such thing as ghosts; of course I'm not afraid.'" There was a murmur of applause and the boy continued naïvely: "I wasn't afraid of the horses either, though they were real enough, so. . . ."

"What's that?" cried Black in sudden excitement. "What horses?"

Instantly the judge and the prosecutor yelled at him in unison and the guard's hand was like iron on his shoulder. This time he would not yield, he was no longer the bewildered Russian peasant but a free-born American fighting for his life. "I have a right to speak," he shouted back, "or is justice all a lie in Soviet Russia? I demand an answer to my question." He stood with hand outstretched towards the judge and their eyes met while the audience roared its fury.

Hard and cruel that judge, and fanatically prejudiced, but a man and a soldier who knew men and courage. He raised his hand and the tumult ceased. He turned to the boy.

"You may answer the question," he said quietly.

The Pioneer's face was blank with surprise. "Who should know better than you, Maxim Maximovich? Were not your own horses among them, five mares and your black stallion, Koshchei?"

The prosecutor sprang to his feet. "I protest; this evidence is irrelevant. I . . ."

Black interrupted him without a qualm. "Did you give me the right or not?" he asked the judge, and the judge, staring hard at him, replied, "I did; go on, boy, finish your answer."

"When we made the Collective, we put all the horses together in the pasture, as common property. Some of the less cultured peasants didn't want Koshchei; they said his hide and his heart were black as his master's name, that he was bad and vicious as a kulak."

Again Black interrupted, "Has the horse, Koshchei, ever attacked anyone?" Now there was no sound in the courtroom as the audience waited eagerly, caught by this sudden blaze of drama.

"Who should know better than you, Maxim Maximovich?" the boy repeated. "You howled like a hurt wolf last year when you had to pay compensation, a whole year's wages, for my Uncle Sergei, because that brute had knocked him down and savaged him." Once more that strange sigh like a distant groan swept the courtroom.

Black shook his fist at the prosecutor. "At last, as you said, we get the truth." Then, turning to the judge, he asked softly, "Does Soviet justice allow that the hoofs of the vicious kulak stallion, Koshchei, be examined carefully, by *you* and by men *you* trust?"

"You insolent dog," said the prosecutor.

"Yes," said the judge, "you shall go and you," pointing to one of the guards and to a middle-aged man in black leather coat and breeches, sitting in the front row. "Take the sidecar and make haste."

"The Court is adjourned for an hour," said the judge.

The audience was abuzz with eager talk when they filed back into court.

"Summon the witnesses," the judge ordered, and the soldier with his black-clad companion came in from behind the prosecutor and stood near his table facing the prisoners. Their faces were hot and flushed and their clothes covered with dust. The soldier was so shaken by excitement that his bayonet quivered visibly. The other man stood motionless, but with a thrill of triumph Black saw that he held a small black satchel in his right hand. Surely. . . .

"Alexei Fomich, make your report," said the judge.

The man in leather took a step forward. "We examined the hoofs of the stallion Koshchei," he said in a low deep voice, "and on both forefeet we found traces of dried blood and hair which corresponds to that of our dead comrade. We removed the horseshoes, which I bring here as evidence." He began to open the satchel.

The judge raised his hand. "Wait," he said. Then to the soldier, "Ivan Nikitch, do you confirm this testimony?"

The soldier stepped forward and saluted. "Yes, Comrade Judge, in every particular."

In silence, save for a rustle as the audience strained forward to

97

watch more closely, the first witness produced the horseshoes and handed them to the judge, who examined them minutely. His two colleagues leaned sideways to look, and the prosecutor came forward to join them. He bent down close to the table, then straightened up, turned back and sat slumped in his seat. Black knew that he was saved.

The judge rang his bell. "No doubt is possible," he said loudly. "Both horseshoes are covered with blood, and a number of hairs adhere to them. Their unusual color and texture makes it certain that they came from the head of our girl comrade. The case of murder against the prisoners is dismissed."

There was not a sound in the crowded room save a deep sigh of relief from the priest, who crossed himself and began muttering. Black sat with arms folded and stared at the judge. Was he wrong or was there a look of respect in his hard blue eyes? The judge whispered briefly to his colleagues. "The case of murder is dismissed," he said, "but the Court has decided to pronounce its verdict immediately. There is no need for us to retire and consider it." He rose to his feet and everyone in the room stood up. "The prisoner Konin, Ivan Petrovitch, is acquitted in virtue of his youth and low cultural level. Let this be a lesson to him for the future.

"The prisoner Grusof, Timofei Timofeich, has been shown guilty of subversive and superstitious utterances and threats against our dead comrade. I sentence him to three years' exile in a prison camp.

"The prisoner Chorny, Maxim Maximovitch, has shown himself to be a kulak of the worst type. I pass over his insolence to my colleagues and his repeated defiance of the Court." Again Black fancied that there was something of respect in the judge's look. "But he too has been guilty of threats against the dead comrade. He has given proof of antisocial individualism and has attempted to hold back the clock of progress. For him and for those like him there is no place in our new society. I sentence him to two years' exile in a prison camp. The court is dismissed."

At the top of the flight of steps leading to their underground cell they were stopped by the young man who had first admitted them to the courthouse. He whispered a moment to the guard, then said to Black: "Go with him. Comrade Fromof, the presiding judge, wishes to speak to you."

The judge was sitting at a desk in a small upper room. He motioned Black to take a chair opposite him and said abruptly: "I want to thank you. You have saved me today from committing an error of justice." He turned to the guard: "You will drive the prisoner Chorny back to Masupovo in the side-car and let him collect food and heavy clothing and say goodby to his family. An exile train will pass through here in three hours; I hold you responsible for the prisoner's delivery at the station."

The soldier talked volubly as the wheezy motorcycle rattled through the ill lit streets, but Black paid little heed. His mind was occupied with one thought only, to locate the ninth milestone, beyond which the egg had fallen. Fortunately, the moon was nearly full and their speed was not more than fifteen miles an hour as they bumped over the ruts and obstacles of the track. The soldier had brought his rifle with fixed bayonet but Black saw with satisfaction that it was slung across his back. At the eighth milestone he had a stroke of luck. They swung across to the left of the track bordering the ditch, where the going was smoother. The sidecar was on the left of the motorcycle, and when they reached the ninth stone Black braced himself for an effort. One post . . . two . . . three. . . . He threw himself bodily out and landed in the ditch, shaken but unhurt.

The soldier gave a loud cry and jammed on his brake. Fumbling frantically in the grass, Black heard the man curse as the machine bucked him from his seat. An instant's glance saw him scramble to his feet and unhitch his rifle. Another shout as the soldier charged, but that very second Black saw a gleam of gold and his fingers closed upon the egg. As he sensed his enemy poised for the blow he gasped, "Wish . . . I . . . home . . . New York . . . as before. . . ."

Once more he was caught in the whirl of darkness and light and . . . he was sitting at his own dinner table still pointing his hand at his nephew.

"If you were a Russian kulak, Uncle Max, perhaps you'd think differently," said the young man.

The banker started, and looked round the room as if unable to believe his eyes. Yes, it was true, he was home again. Drawing a long breath, he filled a port glass with brandy and gulped it down.

"You are right, my boy, perhaps I should."

The Wife Who Lost Her Patience

IN A VILLAGE of the Moscow province not more than sixty miles from the Soviet capital there lived a poor couple, husband and wife, with two girls of fifteen and sixteen, and two small children of five and six. As Russian holdings go, they ranked as "middle" peasants; that is, they had twenty straggling acres, one-third of which was always left idle in the old-fashioned way, a cottage of two rooms, and a sturdy little horse.

Before the war they had lived as well as a peasant could expect; namely, without hunger, except in the bad year of 1911. But Ivan was different when he came back from the army in '19. He had lost the habit of labor, and acquired other habits, less worthy. He neglected his wife henceforth, and dreamt of a gay life; wine, song and women.

Well, there was vodka a-plenty, good strong home brew, at forty kopecks a quart, despite the prohibition law; and always some one to play the concertina in the smoke of the local *traktir*, with a crowd of good fellows full of liquor and revolutionary ballads; and hussies, who helped to squander the rubles wrested from the farm.

The wife, Natalia, bore easily her husband's infidelities. That he came home and beat her seemed natural enough — it was the custom. Men were always like that, and there was nothing to be done about it. The waste of money was less easy to endure. They needed it so badly. The land was tough and sticky, the plow blunt and warped.

And now, under the new regime, just five rubles would make the first payment on a steel plow, with a sharp cutting edge. The Soviet gave good seed grain, too, at a nominal cost. If only Ivan would get the plow, he needn't work hard. She and the girls and the little horse could do all that was needed. Even the babies could sit in the field and wave their arms and cry, to scare away the birds.

To keep the farm going, that was the main thing. To bring the grain up yellow for reaping from the earth, and pile the scented hay into ricks, and store away the potatoes for the winter; to provide a stock of oats to feed the horse until the snow melted and he could graze upon the common, and straw for his bedding — all that she could do without Ivan's help.

They dragged on somehow from year to year, gradually slipping lower, finding it more difficult each season to make ends meet. As the Russian proverb says, "A farm with a bad master is like a team with crossed reins." If Ivan had died, or not come back from the wars, Natalia might have managed. But he was always taking and never giving.

The worst of it was that she could never trust him when he drove into market to sell their grain or hay. There were so many things to be bought, so much needed, Not clothes, or food — they could use what they had; but kerosene, and matches, and salt, and iron nails and tools for the farm. He'd go off with his load, promising to be back before nightfall with everything. And then the sun would set and darkness come, and she would still be waiting. In the morning the horse would pull the sleigh up to the door with the reins hanging on his back, and Ivan lying drunk and redfaced in the straw, stripped of his last kopeck, with nothing to show for it save oaths and blows and an aching head.

One autumn day Ivan drove to town with six sacks of grain to pay his tax and buy what was needed for the winter. The eldest girl, Natasha, now sixteen, begged to go with her father. There was a pattern of cheap print she wanted for a dress, and the market of the little town held for her all the glamor of a city. The mother

102

urged it too, but Ivan refused, at first laughing, then angry. He wouldn't be spied upon, he said. . . . If they didn't trust him — he cursed them in the Russian manner. He was a free man anyway, and he could do as he pleased with what he owned.

He drove off swearing and beating the horse into a gallop. Natalia watched him for a minute, then turned to the girl beside her. "Come on," she said, "it's no good snivelling. We've got to get on with the work. Your father's a man and he knows best."

That night she waited, and all next day, and the night following, but he did not come. Then, just before noon the cart creaked into the muddy yard. Flat in the straw lay Ivan, head resting on a sack of salt, mouth open, face purple, eyes closed, dead drunk.

But where was the horse, the sturdy little horse that worked so well and faithfully? In his place was a poor gaunt creature, all ribs and sores, with weary drooping ears.

Natalia took one look and grabbed her husband by the hair. "Svoloch!" she screamed, shaking his head till his teeth chattered and his eyes opened. "Svoloch! Where is our horse? And where are the goods you promised to bring me?"

The man blinked at her stupidly. "Sold him," he muttered. "Not sold . . . swapped . . . for thish," — he made a feeble gesture with his hand — "and fifteen rubles. This old horse . . . at's all righ' . . . lotsa work shtill . . . good horse. . . . Man mus' have some fun." With a spurt of energy, "S'll righ', m'dear. Didn't forget your salt."

Natalia's lips tightened and she loosed her fingers from his hair. For a moment she stood, then set about unharnessing the wretched nag. When she had led him to the shed and given him oats, she took the bag of salt and put it on the shelf beside the stove in the living-room. Then, with the help of her daughter, she carried her husband in and laid him on the bed, with his head propped on a pillow.

It was now time to make the children's *kasha* and the soup for the older girls. And there was the stubble to pick over and the hay to be loaded on the cart. Their last hope, this hay. She had been right to persuade Ivan not to take it to the town with the grain. Their neighbor, the rich *kulak* Alexei Petrovich, would buy it for his cattle. He had promised her a good price, and through him she might get some of the goods her husband should have brought.

Natasha was sobbing for her lost frock, and the younger girl was whimpering about the leather shoes she had wanted to wear in church on the name day of her saint. But Natalia, silent, worked on.

The little ones played around them in the dusk as the three women piled the load of hay upon the cart. Natasha put them to bed in the smaller room — it was not yet cold enough for them to sleep above the stove beside which their father lay snoring — while Natalia went out to get the horse. The hay must be brought in.

It was nearly dark now, but the moon was rising. She must get this over, she felt, and settled, lest tomorrow her husband should prevent it. That seed grain they must have, and some tools, and stocks for the winter.

She went into the yard and sat close to the horse's tail in the front of the loaded wagon. The poor beast's head hung heavy, but he raised it at her cry and humped his shoulders for the load. The wagon shook but did not move.

In anger Natalia caught his tail and pulled it. The horse whinnied in pain and made another effort. Natalia jumped from her seat and ran to his head. Catching the bridle, she yelled to the smaller girl to beat his rump with a stick, and to Natasha to push the cart.

With starting eyes the horse pulled his hardest. For a second the wheels moved forward, then sogged back into the mud. The animal stood trembling, powerless to move the load. Once more Natalia tugged at the bridle, once more the children beat and pushed, but the horse could not try again. He was worn out. He knew it, and she knew it.

Without word or change of face she took off the harness and led

104

him stumbling to the shed. She told Natasha to give him some more oats, and to rub him down all over with a wisp of straw. "Rub him and rub him," she said. "He's tired now but he'll be better tomorrow." To the smaller girl, too, she gave a task that would take some time. "Carry the hay from the cart into the barn," she ordered her.

Natalia went into the house and took the meat axe from the hook beside the stove. She ran her thumb along its edge. . . .

Aiming straight for the spot above the temple where the veins swelled out from the hair, she swung full weight upon her sleeping husband. The thick blade went deep, but she wrenched it out and struck again savagely; twice, three times, four.

He scarcely moved. Only with the fourth blow his feet drummed a little against the bottom of the bed, and then were still.

Natalia wiped the axe on the blanket and hung it back on its hook. She put her hand upon his heart. No beat. To make sure, she lifted down the mirror and held it against his lips. No breath. Dead like a pig, this *svoloch*. She took in a deep breath, chin up, then brought her head down over the gashed face, and spat.

By the time the girls came in she had got him wrapped from sight in the bloodstained blanket. Both were quiet as she told them what had happened and what must still be done.

The younger girl fetched the two drowsy children into the living-room and soothed them to sleep. Her mother and sister cleared the potatoes from the hole in the ground in the little room and heaped them up against the wall. They carried the body to the hole and laid it in. Above it they spread layer after thick layer of salt, then piled in earth; one foot, two feet, stamping it down flat, and more earth above that until there was no hollow in the floor.

There was little comment in the village on Ivan's disappearance. His wife said that he had probably gone off with one of the hussies from the town. "He's been with them often enough, God knows," she said, "and wasted enough money on 'em." And — they knew

105

the rest that she did not say — hit her in the face when he came home drunk because she was old and ugly.

To the peasants this seemed natural. The fact that Ivan had lived with Natalia nearly twenty years did not enter into it. He had deserted her, but she had the farm so she had nothing to groan about. In fact, it was the general opinion that she was well rid of him. Russian villages worry little about the vagaries of black sheep.

So the life of the farm went on, and Ivan, kept sweet by salt, failed to trouble the sleep of his two small children above him, or of his wife and daughters in the other room.

Well fed with oats, cajoled and beaten, the decrepit horse was able to do the autumn's plowing. The *kulak* neighbor bought the hay and the village soviet gave Natalia seed grain, to which she had a claim, as a woman with four minor children.

Thus they came to the long dark month of December when there is nothing to do on a Russian farm. The girls had almost forgotten their father, so lightly the tragedy touched them. The little ones sometimes asked where Daddy was, and their mother answered that he had gone away.

But Natalia was uneasy in her heart. Not from remorse or fear of spirits of the dead that rise to affright the living. No, no, she knew that Ivan was penned down beneath the barrier of salt — to this day in Soviet Russia salt keeps the mystic values of an earlier age — and three hard-trodden feet of earth.

It was something other. The man had died unshriven in his sin. Even our western litany still keeps alive the old prayer, "From battle and murder and sudden death, Good Lord, deliver us!" to speak the dread of dying without time to repent; the death in sin that dooms the sinner to hell-fire.

The church services at Christmas fixed a plan which had been slowly forming in her mind. Two days later she went to the house of the priest and asked the price of masses for her husband's soul.

Nine masses to bring the chance of salvation to one cut off un-

106

timely would cost five rubles; a great sum for her narrow means. After a moment's struggle she agreed, and gave the priest the money.

The masses were said, but the village wondered. To peasants so starkly poor it was queer and wrong that Natalia should spend five rubles in this way. She told them that she had dreamt her husband's death; had seen him bloated and meshed in weeds at the bottom of a pool; knew her dream was true.

They were not sure. Dreams have meaning, but one does not spend five rubles upon dreams. Gossip spread and a cloud of suspicion blackened. Then one day the officials of the village soviet came to question Natalia.

At first she denied it, but the terror of the girls was plain. A few sharp queries and the facts were known. The two younger children were lodged for the night with the schoolmistress, to be taken later to an orphanage. The body of Ivan was exhumed, and Natalia and her daughters were arrested.

The People's Court of the little township took a simple and practical view. Not long before a woman had poisoned her husband, and local opinion held that female emancipation could be pushed too far.

The court sentenced Natalia to three years in prison. It acquitted the girls as involuntary accessories and ordered them to be sent to a factory training school near by.

Natalia's lawyer, assigned her according to soviet custom from the local panel of the "College of Red Defenders," appealed the verdict to Moscow. The humble origin of his client, the long provocation she had endured, and the existence of four children whose charge now devolved upon the state, would, he felt sure, bring a mitigation of the sentence.

"At the worst," he told Natalia, "you will not have to stay more than a year in prison. But I believe that in the circumstances the Moscow court will make even that penalty conditional."

The Wife Who Lost Her Patience

He was disappointed. True, the Appeal Court found that the woman's act had much to condone it. Her husband had brought his death upon himself by sinning against the first tenets of peasant economy. But there was a graver issue in the case, that of Natalia's superstition.

The court seemed to fear that shortening the sentence might appear as acceptance of "religious ideology." It therefore stated: "The appellant has given proof of gross superstition, and is no fit person to rear her family, as she has also shown by involving two young girls in concealment of the crime. The appeal is dismissed."

The Crazy Poets and the Distant Star

THOSE WHO GUARD great men fear most the assassin who is not wholly sane. From riot and conspiracy they can protect their leaders, but against the lone hand and the addled brain there is no sure defense.

So Booth slew Lincoln and Prinzip the Archduke Ferdinand.

But who knows what cold intelligence may move the weaker minds to action?

The poet Golanov came to Moscow in the spring of '25 from the Crimea, where, he said, he had suffered greatly during the Civil War. A gaunt fellow with freckled face and thick red curls soiling the shoulders of his coat.

He soon became a figure among the younger poets. If at times he spoke harshly of the Revolution, that was not uncommon in the group called "Enthusiasts." They had two grievances against the Soviet State. Their club room, a vaulted cellar in the center of Moscow, had been closed. The Enthusiasts, having no money, had induced a Jewish business man, Moise Ibramovich, to act as manager and run their restaurant.

It was understood that Enthusiast members should have fifty per cent reduction on food and drink, but the friends who came, attracted by their talents, should pay full tariff. Things turned out otherwise. The poet members never paid at all and their guests always produced members' tickets calling for fifty per cent reduction.

Moise Ibramovich was faced by a shocking deficit, which he tried

109

to wipe out by the then illegal sale of vodka. And one fine evening the club was closed.

Their second grievance may have been related to the first. Shortly after the club was shut, their leader, the peasant poet Sergey Essenin, had an altercation with a Jewish citizen in a public place and was arrested. The affair was hushed up but it sowed resentment in poetic circles.

That winter Essenin hanged himself, leaving words of despair scrawled in his own blood, and left his disciples to think of self-destruction.

Golanov doubtless read this, but it was not until he met Tanin that his plans began to shape. Tanin had been one of the three poets arrested with Essenin on account of the anti-Semitic incident; a stocky peasant boy with bright blond hair, fresh color, and sapphire eyes. His poetry was rough but told truth about the land and the peasant, so that for a time they thought he might take Essenin's place.

For Tanin and many of his comrades there was corruption in the city air. They drank and drugged and ran after evil lusts, wasting their talents. In Tanin, who had brooded over Essenin's death, Golanov found his tool.

A new group among the poets was formed under the guidance of these two. There were twelve of them, young men and women, the wildest ones of all, who called themselves "Post-Enthusiasts." They met surreptitiously at night in the cellar of the deserted club. At first they merely drank and sniffed cocaine, and ranted about sex and death and anarchy and God.

Then, when he judged them ripe, Golanov set to work.

A tawdry scene, the dozen satellites humped on the edge of the platform where the orchestra used to play, two candles dripping down bottle necks, and in the middle the lanky Messiah expounding his message of release through death and stars.

This world was evil, he told them, and doomed to perish by

110

pestilence and war. "Look about you," he said. "Everywhere there is ruin and despair. This world is bad and wrong and has corrupted human life like blight on fruit. So we must leave it all behind. In the stars only there is hope for humanity reborn. In the stars and Death."

Then slowly he told his hearers, crazed by theosophy and drugs, how, far in the heavens, there shone the star Capella, symbol of hope for a wasted Earth.

"The doctrine I bring you," he said, "is attainment through sacrifice, eternal joy through mortal pain. There is no hope here for man. He must die by his own will, to be reborn at once in Capella, for a new life of innocence and joy."

He had it all prepared, Golanov. With his brown eyes burning them and his greasy hair adrift across his shoulders. Mass suicide was his gospel, that all humanity should pass in one self-holocaust to a better world beyond the skies. Grotesque and ranting, all of it, but suited to his hearers. And they hung upon his words.

For two weeks he let them dream, with Tanin, now his accolyte, to tend the fire. That Tanin knew then what Golanov aimed at is unlikely. But the clean peasant soul had rotted within him. He was ready to fertilize the field his chief had sown.

Then Golanov made his second move. There was small chance, he said, of world suicide, until a chosen few had shown the way. Always there must be martyrs to a cause, to whom death's face was kind. They twelve must perish sooner that Capella's happiness be known.

With the spell of sacrifice and heaven he wooed them towards death. And Tanin, blue eyes gleaming, whispered to each one of Essenin and suicide, and quick ways of dying.

Always the drugs helped, and the vodka; and the spur of sex, and the folly of loose talk; until he held them in his hand, Golanov, well-balanced for his plan.

For what he fed them next the OGPU killed him. For all they

111

knew, till then he might have been as foolish as the rest, but now he crossed the line.

The Post-Enthusiasts were sitting round a table near the fire-place in the cellar, where they had put one electric lamp. "We are united," Golanov began, "upon our death together, to show the world the way. But there must be no laggards. If one holds back from death, the pact for all is broken and Capella lost. How can we know that one amongst us will not weaken and falter on the brink? That would ruin everything, so we must all be bound that we will surely die."

Voluntary death, of course, but did that mean self-inflicted? He thought not. If they agreed, the way was easy. At the October anniversary of the Revolution there would be a review in the Red Square when the garrison of Moscow, and the workers in drilled ranks, and all the People's Clubs born of the Soviet power would march past the tomb of Lenin under the Kremlin wall.

Wooden steps lead up from the courtyard round the tomb to a platform just below the top. There the rulers of the Soviet State watch the thousands pass.

The Post-Enthusiasts would be marching with the poets. And each of them would have a hand-grenade which he would give them, two pounds of high explosive and hard steel.

"Just press a little hinge," he said, "and count five slowly, and pitch it up onto the platform where they will stand — Rykov, Stalin, Bukharin and the rest. They will be killed, of course. And then, comrades, we also will die quickly. But that is the road to Capella, and before they shoot us — they shall hear the truth."

He had them now, caught in his hoax of paradise and death. Essenin had died alone, but this, they said, was better, a bloody portent for the world to see. Themselves, they were burnt out, and knew too much too young. This would be a fine resounding end, like a sunset, or the crash of thunder.

112

The Crazy Poets and the Distant Star

So they shouted their consent. And Golanov, the gaunt spider, went off to get the bombs.

The OGPU never knew who his friends were, but they believed the bombs were ready and that the plot failed only by a fluke.

The Post-Enthusiasts met for the last time when the days were shortening towards the October celebration. Cocaine and death and life in the stars and vodka kept them talking late into the night. At the end Golanov and Tanin sat talking together under the lamp near the hearth. The cellar had arches and pillars, like a church, so that shadows from the single light deepened into blackness.

The rest of the group were sprawled over the platform, far from the fireplace, outside the circle of light. Their excitement had died, the effect of their drugs worn off, and they were quiet. Perhaps they were bored or felt neglected. Some fell asleep, as Golanov and Tanin talked on.

At last one of them woke and roused the others. "Watch me," he said to them. "Has anyone got a match?"

They gave him a box and he put some matches between his teeth. He lay down upon the floor and began to crawl slowly forward. After he had gone a few feet he stopped and took the matches from his mouth. "Keep quiet," he whispered, "and watch me. It will be very funny."

They were wide awake now, this crazy company, and sat bending forward in eager silence. Under the lamp Golanov and Tanin talked and gestured, their voices a steady murmur.

Stealthily the boy crawled round the pillars, keeping always in shadow. It must have been five minutes before they saw his head move forward into the light, directly behind Golanov. His shoulders followed, and then his whole body, silently, inch by inch. Now he was crouching behind Golanov's chair, in his hand a lighted match. He raised his hand with breathless caution, and touched the match to the leader's long dank hair.

For a moment they waited. Then with fizz and splutter the man's

113

whole head was in a flame. Behind him the jester danced, and his friends on the platform kicked their heels and screamed with laughter.

Golanov leapt up in torture, his arms beating at his head. They shouted the louder. Was there ever a joke like this? They clapped their hands, and called, "Fire!" and "Water! Water!"

Tanin heard them and understood. He plunged forward and knocked the practical joker face down into the fireplace, then whirled and seized a bottle and flung it at the yelling crew.

Frenzied with rage and pain, Golanov caught up a chair and rushed them, striking right and left. At once it was pandemonium. Howls and cries and curses, wild battle in the dark, each grappling the nearest shadow, raving for blood.

A girl stood rigid against the wall, her mouth fixed open, shrieking one high dreadful note, like the scream of a horse. That cry reached a militiaman on the street corner and shocked him from his doze. He jumped and ran forward, blowing furiously on his whistle.

It took ten men to get them to the police station, and only when more than half of them had been clubbed senseless. The rest raved, as the drug madness, revived by the battle, racked their nerves. The girl who had screamed began to chant over and over the refrain, "After we've thrown our bombs, we'll mount beyond the skies."

They could not help but hear, and the word "bomb" has its own grim potency in Moscow. They listened again, then telephoned the OGPU.

An official hurried to the police station, for they who guard the Kremlin's lords can overlook no sign. That night he heard enough to warrant an inquiry. For days afterwards he played them one by one with their drugs withheld or granted, until he had it all.

There was no public trial. The OGPU is empowered to handle emergencies. The lesser Post-Enthusiasts were sent to hospital to be set free when cured.

114

The Crazy Poets and the Distant Star

Golanov and Tanin were executed. Tanin seemed to know nothing of what might lie behind the poets' death pact, but they judged him dangerous and sane enough for shooting.

Golanov's case was less simple. The OGPU examiners were convinced that he was more than a fanatic. They found he had belonged to a Terrorist group in the Crimea, where he had once been arrested for complicity in a campaign of assassination. There had been no proof against him and he was released, and passed from sight until he appeared in Moscow. They believed that he was connected with foreign elements hostile to the Soviet.

Madman or cunning plotter, he refused to speak, and took his secret with him past the firing squad.

Conspirators

THE MAN at the desk stroked his black beard with caressing fingers. There was eogism in the gesture, thought Zubof, watching. Something reminded him of Assyrian kings as he looked at the dark hair waving back from the high forehead, the hooked nose, heavy lips and arrogant jaw; and the fierce Oriental eyes, so different from those of the Jews Zubof used to know, passive and meek toward their Russian masters. The Revolution had changed that. This man, middle-aged, dominant, was president of the Petrograd Organization Bureau of the Communist party. Zubof, the young Nordic, sat like a schoolboy waiting his orders. He looked out of the window, where the falling leaves were a presage of snowflakes soon to come. It was September of 1919, that cruel year of hunger and Civil War.

The Jew signed the last of a pile of documents, stroked his beard again, and said in a voice so friendly that the young man felt uneasy, "Forgive me, my dear comrade. Sorry to keep you waiting. We have excellent reports of your work in the country."

Zubof knew that he ought to say he was honored, but no words came.

"Unless I'm mistaken" — the voice was too smooth — "you've been a member of the Party since April 1917. Your father was a landlord near Pskov, and you lived there until you were twenty. Yes?"

"Yes, a landlord," Zubof stammered. "But I didn't keep it, the land. I knew how wrong — this exploitation. I gave it back to the peasants voluntarily — "

116

"I'm not blaming you for your father's position," broke in the other. "Your revolutionary record is excellent, and we have every confidence in you. Otherwise you wouldn't be here."

The harsh note at the end somehow made Zubof feel more comfortable.

"But you know the people thereabouts, most of them?" the Jew asked.

"Yes," said Zubof, puzzled.

"There's been a lot of trouble in these border provinces, what with the Estonian war and Yudenich's White Guard army — you may know Yudenich is going to drive at Petrograd one of these days — and English cruisers banging guns to frighten old women. But they can't beat us that way. If only . . . The Red Army, if only it were red! But we're not solid. And down there in Pskov, the key point, the railroad junction, right on the Estonian border, there's conspiracy — White Guards, English money, Estonians, Social Revolutionary traitors."

He paused and glared at Zubof.

"I don't understand," the young man ventured.

"Of course not; forgive me, my dear comrade." The voice was bland again. "You see, we have trailed these conspirators on our own Russian soil. An Extraordinary Commission has been appointed to investigate, with our very good Comrade Galkin in charge. But Galkin, like all of us, has been desperately overworked. Yesterday he fainted. They couldn't revive him. They took him to a hospital. Now he's been ordered absolute rest for a fortnight. You're to take on his job."

Zubof was bewildered.

The Jew bent forward and signed another document. "This is a mandate appointing you head of the Extraordinary Commission to investigate, with full powers, the conspiracy in the region of Pskov."

Then Zubof understood. He had been made an executive of the Cheka.

117

Conspirators

He sprang from his chair. "Oh, Comrade! This isn't my line at all! I can organize the peasants; you admitted I did my job well. And I can fight; on the Samara front my company lost eighty-five men out of two hundred, and I got a bullet in my shoulder. I have papers to prove it. But I'm no police spy, no provoc — "

The Jew seized his wrist.

"Stop! There's no talk of police spies or provocation. You are required to examine these people and judge them and — "

"I'm no grand inquisitor, either! It's no good; you must find — "

"Stop! I tell you! And listen to me. You are not here to argue, but to take orders which you will obey. The Party has decided you can be useful in a certain position. How dare you question that decision? You say you have commanded men in battle; what would you think of a soldier who — "

"Why, if the Party ordered Lenin himself to — "

"You young fool," said the other more quietly. "The matter is settled. You have never worked for the Cheka; very well, you begin today. There are a dozen people here under arrest, probably most of them known to you, as they come from your home neighborhood. Find out those who are guilty and have them shot at once. If any are innocent, let them go free. Above all, act quickly; that is the principle of the Terror. Your predecessor, Comrade Galkin, promised to have it all finished by tomorrow night."

Zubof's face was pale, but his resistance was smashed. He took the mandate, saluted and left the room.

Twenty-two is an elastic age, not overprone to quarrel with sudden promotion. When Zubof jumped from the automobile before the small, square building that once had housed the darling of a millionaire contractor, his dismay had become pride.

There was a sweet savor in the quick salute of the sentries, and in the deference that met him as he entered the anteroom leading to

118

his private office. It had been a sort of Cubist studio. The walls were a patchwork of orange, blue and green framed in bars of black; the floor a checkerboard of black and white marble; the ceiling a stained-glass dome. In all this color, the black leather tunics and breeches of the three secretaries seemed perverse and dreadful.

The inner room, which was formerly the lady's boudoir, was like a jewel case. Its silk panels of pale fawn were flushed by the light from a bowl of pink marble. The carpet was white, thick and soft as moss, but a strip of red baize ran across it from the door to an ivory table. Even the telephone cord was white, and the box on which the receiver rested had been coated with creamy paint.

"Comrade Galkin must be a strange person," thought Zubof, as he sat down in the high-backed ivory chair behind the table.

There was a tap at the door, and a little elderly man with a leather portfolio came forward, stepping carefully on the narrow red strip. His assured manner was that of the smaller officials Zubof had known, living on modest pensions in the country.

With a murmur, "Egor Nikich; at your service, Comrade," he sat down at the table and began to explain the work in hand, referring from time to time to the typed papers in his portfolio.

The conspiracy, it appeared, was for the purpose of blowing up a railway bridge near the important junction of Pskov, and at the same time rousing the country against the Bolsheviki. The conspirators had been in touch with the counter-revolutionary army of Yudenich, and with the "Green Bands," who were in theory anti-Bolshevist patriots, but in practice marauding bandits who had heard the clink of foreign money. Once the bridge was out, they would sweep down from the northwest and the Estonians would attack from the west and south.

The plans had been revealed by an accident, about which Egor Nikich knew little. At any rate, the leaders had been caught. The

119

bridge was guarded, two battalions were moving in, and a military tribunal would soon reassure the local population.

There remained only the execution of justice on the chief conspirators. Perhaps, the secretary said, not all the prisoners in hand were equally guilty; but there was no doubt that the motive force of the conspiracy was among them. Comrade Zubof would apportion their guilt and pass judgment. The sentences would be carried out at once. In fact, Comrade Galkin had hoped to finish the whole —

"All right," interrupted Zubof. "I'll begin now; see them one at a time. You stay outside and send them in."

Egor Nikich tiptoed out along the red baize strip.

When one is young, and tender of heart, it is no light thing to condemn one's fellow creatures to sudden death. Zubof braced himself to do his duty. They had plotted against the revolution. He must have no false sentiment. He must show —

There was a burst of exclamations at the door, and a tall, stout woman was pushed into the room.

Severe and rigid, Zubof waved her to a seat before the desk. The model judge, he felt, should be impassive, without animosity.

His gesture was hardly finished when the prisoner flung herself upon him with a squeal of delight, and kissed him on both cheeks.

"Vassia, my little Vassia! It is really you!"

Zubof's brain swam. This first of his dangerous plotters was Tatiana Ivanova — Aunt Tania, one of his mother's friends. His relation to her had been fixed one October afternoon years ago, when she had caught young Vassia, who was then about ten, robbing her orchard for the sake of small Kyra, the seven-year-old daughter of the commanding officer of the district. For himself, Vassia would never have stolen a button; but it was the old story — Eve wanted the apple.

On that October day their present roles had been reversed. Aunt Tania had executed summary justice with the palm of her

120

hand. He had yelled and kicked in vain. His young accomplice had said that she did not like little boys who cried, and had left him. In that moment the boy tasted the first pangs of unsuccessful sin. And from the day he kept a respectful fear of Aunt Tania, though he was grateful for her kindness in his mother's last illness.

He persuaded the agitated lady to sit down, but his judicial mien could not be recaptured. Aunt Tania gave him no chance. She burst into thanks to Heaven that at last she had found her little Vassia. How pale he was looking, and how thin! How hard he must be working! What would his poor mother think, to look from Heaven and see him in such a position! And those dreadful Bolsheviki, what did they mean by arresting her and taking her away before she could pack up anything?

" — and you know, Vassia, I always do my best for the peasants. How much wine and soup and all I have given them, ungrateful creatures! And their prisons are so dirty. Vermin, actually, Vassia! And horrible black bread!"

And as she was a living woman, only one change of linen in three weeks, and little chance to wash anything. She did not ask for much in days like these, but at least, if she had to meet her God, she would like to meet him clean and decent.

Zubof could not stem the torrent until she stopped for breath.

"Yes, yes, I know," he said. "But look here, Aunt Tania" — the term slipped out in spite of him — "we must consider this seriously. I have an important duty to do. It appears you have been mixed up in a serious business."

He tried to speak sternly, but memory brought the picture of a small, kicking boy firmly held on that ample knee, minus — supreme indignity — his trousers, with a small, scornful Eve in the background.

Tatiana Ivanova pulled herself together. Thrusting out an angry chin, she said in a hard tone, "You don't mean to tell me, Vassia, that you believe this nonsense! There was I, living quietly, and the

121

good God knows it's hard enough to live in these days with money of no value and prices beyond reason! And suddenly, in the middle of the night, a lot of hulking rogues, drunk, half of them I am sure, burst in and told me I was arrested; that I must go at once to Petrograd. I gave them a piece of my mind, I can tell you; and after that they behaved a little better. But I had to sit in a dirty third-class compartment with a soldier puffing *mahorka* in my face, and since then . . . I cannot tell you. It makes me sick. But if your dear mother could see what is happening, poor saint that she is, she would not be happy, even in Heaven."

Zubof was thinking that it was unlikely that the old lady, the widow of a small official, living quietly on her tiny estate, could be mixed up in an important conspiracy. She had a fondness, he remembered, for interfering in other people's affairs, and she was a bit of a gossip; but her charity and Christian virtue were a pattern to the neighborhood.

For form's sake he questioned her. Had she been in touch with anti-Bolshevik elements? What about the "Green Bands?" Had she ever sent messages to Reval? And so on.

Again he was overwhelmed by a flood of words. What had a poor widow to do with politics and conspiracies? She lived in her own house, if that was a crime nowadays. She had even kept a few gold pieces, and her cook had refused to leave her. Was that a crime? She had written to her brother's wife in Reval. Was it a crime to write to one's own relatives? But she knew Vassia understood all this. Vassia had education; and if he was working for the Bolsheviks, at least he could not share their blind prejudice against anyone who had once owned land. Vassia himself had owned land. He had made a great mistake; she had told him what would come of it if he gave it back to those ungrateful peasants. And see what was happening! In these days, landlords must stick —

The old lady checked herself and burst into tears, calling upon a number of saints, among whom Zubof's mother was most promi-

122

nent, to protect her. His mother knew the truth, she could see, sobbed Aunt Tania. She must even now be praying for mercy for her unhappy son.

Zubof could bear it no longer. At the worst, the old woman was a busybody. She had perhaps talked unwisely. But there was no harm in her; he knew that.

He seized a pen and filled in a mandate from the little book at his elbow. "Citizen Tatiana Ivanova Kouznetsof is released unconditionally. By order of the Extraordinary Commission; Investigating Officer, Zubof."

He scratched his name and stamped the seal of the Cheka in red on the paper. "All right, Aunt Tania," he said, "I am sure you have had nothing to do with this business. But for heaven's sake be more careful. It is not only what you do that matters, but what you say. Of course our people are suspicious. Why, there may be fighting on the northwest front at any moment. Try to be careful."

He cut her thanks short by ringing the little bell of jade that lay on the ivory table. Egor Nikich came in.

"I have decided to release this prisoner," said Zubof. "Here is the mandate. You will see to it. Kindly send in the next."

Zubof drew a long breath as the door closed behind the triumphant lady. He felt physically weak. This was not what he had expected. He sat for a few moments, trying to remember the importance of his mission; the need to be cool, careful, impartial.

His mind flashed back to a picture he had once seen in an illustrated magazine of an English judge, stern and dignified in his old-fashioned robes. So he tried to see himself. But the setting was impossible! The boudoir of a naughty lady was far removed from the Gothic dignity of Westminster Abbey, or wherever it was that the English tried their prisoners. Nevertheless, the idea held him. He pressed the jade button.

123

Conspirators

The next prisoner was a middle-aged peasant with a brown beard, dull round face, and piglike eyes under a low forehead wrinkled with fear and mistrust. He wore a dirty coat of sheepskin with the wool outside. As he shuffled across the strip of carpet in his heavy felt boots, his arms hanging and his red fingers emerging like bundles of sausages from his greasy sleeves, there came a stench of stable and sweat. As he stood swaying a little before the desk, Zubof recognized him: Dmitri Feodorovich Ozol.

Dmitri had a small farm on the property of one of Zubof's mother's friends. In the old days he had been in trouble several times for stealing game, and once he had been imprisoned as a result of a struggle with the gamekeeper. Zubof remembered that the village priest had complained that the man was a wife-beater, and more than usually drunk. It was suspected, too, that he made illicit vodka. A pretty bad lot, thought Zubof; just the man to turn a dishonest penny by acting as messenger in an affair like this.

If Ozol recognized his judge, he gave no sign.

Without speaking, Zubof looked quickly through the prisoner's dossier. Ah! Known to have made frequent trips across the Estonian border without permit, on several occasions bringing back a heavily loaded cart. Nothing ascertained as to contents. Reason to believe him engaged in traffic in arms. Explanations unsatisfactory, uncorroborated. Seemed to have plenty of money. Declined to speak when arrested. Noted by arresting officer as highly suspicious.

Zubof looked up and said severely: "You have been caught red-handed. We know all about you and what you have been doing. Your life is properly forfeit. Your only chance of saving it is to tell freely what you know, who employed you, and the names of the people you saw in Estonia."

The other looked at him blankly.

"Come on, man, speak up. I have no time to waste with you. Tell me at once who paid you."

124

Conspirators

Still no answer. The peasant moistened his thick red lips with the tip of his tongue. His little eyes glanced anxiously round the room.

Again Zubof saw the stern English judge in his robes at Westminster. His manner became more judicial.

"I shall count five," he said, "and if you have not answered, it will go hard with you."

Stretching out a threatening forefinger, he began, "One — two — three — "

The man gulped and bent forward, putting his hands on the table. "I have done nothing," he said thickly. "Nobody paid me. I do not know what it is all about."

"You know that you went across the border with your horse and cart. You know how many times you went. You know whom you saw, and what you brought back. Speak now — quickly!"

The prisoner opened his mouth, and shut it again. He tried once more. He exploded in one word, "Contraband!"

A thrill of triumph ran through Zubof. Ah! This was the way to handle them.

"Yes," he said sternly, "contraband. And what kind of contraband? And where did you get it?"

"Good stuff," was the reply. "None of your dirty *samagon*, but fully sixty per cent; good corn liquor from the big distillery in Reval."

Suddenly a torrent of words came: "My brother, he lives in Reval and he was working in the distillery and the boss said to him, 'Michael Feodorovich, we aren't doing any business here. There aren't enough people in all this wretched little country to buy the stuff we make. We have got to sell more of it. Russia's the place, my boy. They must be pinched tight as a harness over there. What about that good-for-nothing brother of yours there?' he said. He said, 'You get hold of him, Misha. We will make a little piece of change.'

125

Conspirators

"So Misha sent me a message. He said it was no use bringing out money to exchange, because of the money being different now and only paper anyway and worth nothing — God knows life is hard enough without that — so I was to bring things that came from the big houses — carpets or chairs or silver samovars or plates. Well, Barin, I got hold of some of that and took it over and we swapped it for the liquor, and it was good business. Even the president of the soviet bought it, and he kissed me on both cheeks and said I was a fine fellow, and the priest, too, and he had never liked me before, and everybody. And I went two or three times again, and everybody was happy, and then suddenly along come these soldiers."

The man's volubility made a bad impression on Zubof. He remembered similar protestations of innocence from Ozol, when half a dozen plump pheasants had been found under some straw in his stable. Zubof knew he was stubborn, and would stick to the stupid tale.

For the sake of fairness he asked some further questions. As he had expected, there was little variation. It was without much compunction that he sent the man out. He meant to order his execution as soon as the investigation was finished. The man was clearly guilty, but he might need to talk with him again.

Zubof pressed the button for the third time. After a moment, he heard quick, light steps coming across the anteroom. The door opened, and before him stood the one person he had no thought of seeing, Kyra, the playmate of his childhood. He had thought her far from Revolution and its changes, in her school in Paris.

She stopped short at sight of him. "Vassia!"

Again he felt that pang of intolerable loss that he had known three years ago. Somehow he steadied himself.

"Well, Vassily Petrovich, this is a nice mess!" The commonplace

126

words, spoken with a little smile, half nervous, half appealing, brought Zubof back to reality.

"Sit here, please, Kyra Nicolaevna," he said formally, "while I read through these notes."

Shading his eyes as if from the light, he glanced at his prisoner. She was prettier than ever, with bobbed golden hair, pansy-blue eyes, and a graceful figure. Zubof forced himself to look at the page before him. Suddenly the phrases shocked him.

"Arrested in the company of two men and one woman, all former aristocrats. This group attempted armed resistance, in which two of the officials and the prisoner's three companions were killed."

The report was long, and damning enough. The prisoner had returned illegally from France at the beginning of 1919, and had lived some time in Petrograd under an assumed name. Three months previously she had appeared in the neighborhood of Pskov, where she was born and where her father had formerly been a landlord. She was known to have made several trips to Reval, once in company with the prisoner Ozol. Had fired a revolver at the head of the arresting officer, narrowly missing him. In company with the three prisoners killed was undoubtedly a ringleader of the plot.

Zubof could not master his thoughts. They returned to a child in a pansy-blue cap that matched her eyes, watching him struggle on the lap of Aunt Tania. He thought of a slim girl in a St. Petersburg drawing-room, looking up at him from under her long lashes, a pitiful quiver at the corners of her mouth, as the old general shouted, "Say goodby now, and make an end of it. Once for all, young man, I tell you plainly, no daughter of mine shall marry a revolutionary, a traitor to the Czar." .

He thought of the lonely days that followed, the growing despair until he had thought he could not go on living. Perhaps it was his anger at her father's intolerance that had made him decide to live.

Revolutionary, was he? He'd show them, all of the . . . At least it had helped him to forget.

Suddenly it came to him that the passion he had thought stifled was as strong as ever. It was too much to bear. Too much!

He pulled his thoughts back to the white room. "My poor Kyra," he said, "I cannot tell you how dreadful all this is to me."

"Yes, but you don't think I am . . . I mean . . . But what are you doing here, Vassia? I simply cannot understand it."

Zubof's hand shook as he lit a cigarette. "You see," he said, "I always had a different viewpoint, other ideas. Naturally you think as your father thinks, I understood that when he sent you to France. You will never know how I suffered. I'll tell you the truth. I thought of suicide. You never wrote —"

Kyra lifted her hand and tried to speak, but Zubof stopped her.

"But I was angry; that helped. Your father called me a revolutionary because I had liberal ideas. Why should I enjoy the fruit of other men's labor just because I was the son of my father? You didn't see it, nor the general. . . . The old order has passed. Now I am given this work here. You must understand that I will do my duty without regard to anything in my earlier life."

To his amazement the young woman laughed.

"Oh, Vassia," she said. "You are wonderful! You make me quite frightened."

Zubof felt like a man who reaches the top of a staircase, thinks there is another step and finds that there is not.

"You don't understand," he said. "This is serious. And I must ask you not to call me Vassia."

The girl's face, pale a few minutes before, was smiling. She seemed to be blind to the gravity of her position; to see herself simply as a young and attractive female, meeting again a young man she had enslaved long ago.

"Vassia," she said, "do you remember the first time I ever saw you?"

The investigator of the Cheka felt the red come into his face. What devils women were! Didn't the girl understand that her life was at stake?

"I'm afraid you don't yet understand what is facing you," he said.

The girl's face changed. It hurt him to see how forlorn she looked.

"Yes," she said. "But where is Gal — I mean, what are you doing here?"

Zubof hardened. "I am here by orders to replace a comrade who is ill. Really, Kyra," he dropped back into the old familiar manner, "you must keep to the matter in hand."

To his surprise, the girl said, "Then you are here only temporarily?"

"I don't understand why you are asking."

"Oh well," said Kyra, wearily, "what is it that you want to say to me?"

"Unfortunately there is not much to say," said Zubof gently. "The case against you is too clear. You will have to understand that our old friendship is nothing now, that I must do my duty. I must not think of those old days. All I have got to decide is whether you are guilty or not. I give you the same chance to speak that I would give to anybody else. I do not blame you. With your bringing-up, your view of life, it was natural that you should feel as you do. But that doesn't change it. You are guilty of counter-revolution."

For a moment they looked at each other, the girl pale, swaying a little with weakness or fatigue, the man curious, troubled unyielding. Then her eyes fell. "Do you mean to say," she whispered, "that you think I am guilty?"

Zubof nodded. "I know you are guilty. I — I must judge you."

She looked at him long and searchingly. Then her manner changed.

129

Conspirators

"Very well, Vassily Petrovich," she said, "I must tell you. You have grown up since I last saw you, but I'm afraid you'll be startled. I hate to tell you, because I can see that you don't understand this kind of work, and you probably despise it. But — the fact is — I am a revolutionary. Galkin knows all about me. The truth is that I am working for him as a secret agent. He might never have known anything about all this business if I had not told him."

For a moment Zubof was startled. He caught himself. Of course she knew Galkin's name. That meant nothing. The rest was absurd and pathetic. He pressed the button.

"Egor Nikich," he said to the little clerk, without looking at the girl, "do you know this young woman?"

The clerk stared. "It is one of the prisoners," he said, "who have been here four days now. I brought her in twice to speak to Comrade Galkin."

"Yes, yes, I know," broke in Zubof. "But do you know anything else about her?"

"Of course not, Comrade," said Nikich, growing fearful. "I have never seen her before in my life. I know nothing about her except the facts as I have recorded them."

"But she says she knows Comrade Galkin," persisted Zubof. "She says that she is his agent, that she was working to show up the conspiracy."

The clerk was struck with panic. "Upon my word, Comrade Zubof, I know nothing. I cannot believe it. She has been treated like the rest of the prisoners. Comrade Galkin could have nothing to do with counter-revolution."

Zubof turned to Kyra.

"You hear that?" he said.

The girl paled.

"All right," she said. "I suppose he doesn't know, this little man. Go ahead, Comrade Zubof. Decide as you think fit. But if not for

130

my sake, then for the sake of the cause you serve, consult Comrade Galkin before you finish.''

She walked towards the door. The clerk followed her, and the door closed.

Zubof put his elbows on the desk and tried in desperation to think it out. Of course he could not consult Galkin. With his full powers he had been given full responsibility. And the doctors had said that Galkin must not be disturbed. . . .

His mind leaped away. Something sweet and precious had come back to him. He half rose, his eyes eager. He must tell her! What madness! He dropped back into the ivory chair. This girl, this golden center of his life, a criminal, guilty beyond doubt. . . . For him, her judge, there was only to pass sentence . . . sentence . . . sentence. . . .

He thought of the stories he had heard of Cheka executions — the blank courtyard, deep and narrow as a well, in the center of the high dark building; the lantern held so that its light might fall on the figure leaning against the wall; the gleam of leveled rifles and the shadows of the men; at the side, quivering, the great truck with open exhaust sending crashes of sound against the steep wall.

No! He could not bear it. He dashed through the anteroom and into the street. Deaf to the shout of the soldier in his automobile, he ran along the pavement, driven by horror.

It was midnight when the young man stumbled upstairs to his apartment. He fell forward beside the bed, without knowing that he had fallen.

As the drug of physical fatigue wore away, one idea beat louder than the rest. There was one escape, the one which had offered release three years ago. But to kill himself was not to save Kyra! Kyra must die. That he could not live after that did not matter.

The blood coursed back to his brain, and a new train of reasoning came. She must die, and he; their short lives had been linked for this

131

end by some black destiny. His armor of materialistic Marxism was shattered by the hammer of Slavic fatalism. A few quick breaths of pain or pleasure, effort and achievement, failure and despair. . . . Why, and to what end? Useless to ask . . . *nichevo.* . . . He fell asleep.

He woke late, relieved and strangely peaceful. There was disapproval in the sentry's face as he entered the square house, and a note of reproach, as Egor Nikich said, "We've been wondering what happened to you, Comrade Zubof. You went away in such a hurry. You didn't even give us your address." Then he whispered, "He's come back again. He wanted to see you. He doesn't like to be kept waiting."

"Who?" asked Zubof.

"Comrade Galkin. He came in at nine o'clock and asked for you. You weren't here."

The clerk opened the door of the inner room and announced, "Comrade Zubof."

Behind the desk, perched on the high ivory chair, was a figure so tiny, so neat, that it seemed like a mannikin. The little blue eyes were bright, the lips full and scarlet, but the voice deep and assured. With a wave of the hand, he said, "Come in, Comrade; and please be careful not to walk on the white carpet."

So this was the meaning of the red baize, thought Zubof, as he saluted and came forward.

Galkin regarded his manicured nails. "You are late, Comrade. I was able to return — these stupid doctors; always mistaken! Explain what you have done."

Zubof had only one subject in his mind.

"She is guilty," he said. "I have decided to have her shot."

"You will forgive me, Comrade, if I fail to follow," came the soft reply. "Explain."

"Kyra Nicolaevna," said Zubof.

132

The little man polished his nails against his cheek. "And the others?"

"Tatiana Ivanova I released. She has been stupid and indiscreet, but she is not capable of conspiracy. The peasant Ozol is a subordinate, but he is deep in it. He must be shot. I have not yet seen the rest, but there is no doubt that Kyra is the head of the whole plot."

There, it was over. He could face the future — the short future that was left to him.

"A young man of remarkable acumen, admirably qualified to take my place," murmured Galkin. Then his temper broke. "Don't you know anything, you idiot?" he shouted. "The fools, to send me a cub like this, a numskull, a clodhopper, a soldier! That girl is the best agent I've ever had, the only one who can go everywhere, meet them all on their own ground!

"I don't care about that gossiping old beldam. She's guilty as hell, but we can catch her again. I've seen the peasant myself. Oh, yes, he's guilty, too — of smuggling vodka. But Kyra, my best agent — to think that you . . . Get out of here! Get back to your farm, back to your stupid army!"

Zubof stumbled from the room.

Egor Nikich looked at him with pity; he had overheard. The sentry's salute was halfhearted.

They knew him for what he was, Zubof thought; a fool, an incompetent, a failure. They thought him drowning in a flood of humiliation.

To their amazement his back was straight and his face confident and bright, and he smiled as he waved goodby. There was no room in his mind for shame or plots or even for the Party. All his thought was of Kyra, saved for life and love.

Lucky in Love

ONE DREARY NIGHT in Moscow I sat and thought about this Bolshevik experiment, and what it had cost in tears and pain and blood: and what it meant in hope, or might mean, to Man's future. Was it worth trying, I wondered, or was anything worth while anyway?

One feels like that sometimes in Moscow in the winter, when the nights are always cold and often dreary. Unless, of course, one's a Communist, which doubtless makes a difference.

Then I thought, perhaps Communists feel it, too, if they have any feelings. I daresay they don't feel anything; they just act instead. "Acts, not words," Foch said, but Lenin proved words were acts.

Then I thought of some Anarchists I had met, like Bill Shatoff and his friend in Alma-Ata, the little town way off on the edge of China, where Trotsky was exiled in 1928–29, and wondered whether *they* felt or acted.

Bill Shatoff built the Turksib Railroad from Alma-Ata to Semipalatinsk in Siberia — that's why I went to Alma-Ata in 1930, to witness the "meeting of steel" on the line at a point called Aina-Bulak, a hundred miles further north.

I don't think Bill Shatoff feels much. He just acts, like a Communist, and builds railroads and drives men, drives them all day long and all night, too. Bill said they had to shut the office windows at Alma-Ata because the nightingale made such a row in the evenings. They worked nights on the Turksib, they had no time to sleep; or if they slept, they acted in their sleep. Yes, indeed, they

134

acted; everyone in the town just had to act with Shatoff driving them. But they built the road ahead of time.

Everyone in Alma-Ata was busy those days except Trotsky, who once had more action than all of them. He knew the use of words, too, whether words are acts or not. But they wouldn't let Trotsky act any more, or talk any more, in Alma-Ata. They kept him there until all the talk and action inside of him reached a full head of steam. Then they pushed him out abroad to blow it off, like steam or hot air. Perhaps now they regret they did so.

"Trotsky was out of luck," said Shatoff's friend, the other American Anarchist, the younger one. "Luck does count, counts more than brains sometimes, or the work you do. Look at me, I'm lucky — always was, like the Young Luckinvar the song's about."

To this day I don't know whether that was a terrible pun or meant seriously. He used the phrase often, "like Young Luckinvar," and once added, "who was lucky in everything — love and war, too, that's what the song says," so I remain puzzled.

"It began," he said, "when I was in America in '18, when I jumped the country just about a minute ahead of ten years in Leavenworth. Ten years, mind you, and I dodged it by inches, that's luck, ain't it? I worked across on a freighter to Stockholm, that was in the summer, and got from there to Leningrad — Petrograd, they called it then — and don't ask me how. But I was Young Luckinvar all the time, and it kept right on. They let me into the army without a word, and sent me off to Siberia to fight that Kolchak outfit, and lousy swine they were." He paused and spat on the floor.

That was a dirty war, I tell you, no rules nor regulations, everything went, from biting to gouging. Some of the Whites were devils; they didn't only kill their prisoners — they tortured them. One of the worst was that Cossack fellow, Semyonof, who put captured Reds on a slow fire. His troops caught me once, caught me right, five of them with guns, in a room with a girl. You bet they caught us, and the girl knew what it meant and yelled her head off. Lord, how she yelled! I'd liked her up till then but she yelled so much it made me sick. I mean, why couldn't she keep quiet and not give them the satisfaction of seeing how scared she was. I'd yell when the flame bit me; yes, I'd yell then, I suppose. Yell from pain if you like, but not from fright. A man can't beat pain but he can beat fright. Men are weak and women are weaker, and that's as it should be or we'd get no kick from protecting them, but I couldn't protect this dame of mine. After all, I couldn't blame the girl for yelling; I'd have yelled myself if I'd have thought it would have done me any good, instead of giving aid and comfort to the enemy, as they say.

So there we were, with these lousy Cossacks grinning like the wolf in the fairy tale before they started to eat us — and worse — when in burst a Red Army boy and started shooting. That gave me a chance to jump for my gun in the corner and join the game. We shot them up all right, all five of them, and came out without a scratch. The tables were turned, as you might say; the surprise was on them this time, and it was all over in a minute. He was a friend in need, I tell you, and that was how I first met him, the best friend I ever had, my friend Alexei.

After we'd thrown what was left of the Cossacks out in the snow, I said to him, "Thank you, Comrade. You came just in time. How'd you hear about it?" He said a peasant told him, and he couldn't wait for the rest of his outfit; he just came quick.

"Where," I said, "did you learn to shoot like that?"

He laughed, "Oh, that was point-blank stuff, not shooting. You shoot pretty good yourself, but the next time you have a party of this kind take my advice and put your gun under the pillow because you may need it quick. Always put it under the pillow so that you can get it when you need it; that's the best place to put it."

This Alexei and me, we fought together on that front and later in the Crimea against Wrangel, and in '22 near Khiva in the Basmachee trouble. We were always good friends and became better

136

and better friends. A girl can't be friends with you the way a man can; I mean you'd *kill* for the girl, but you'd *die* for a man. Alexei was the best friend I ever had.

"Oh," he said to me one day, "you're a lucky guy, Ed; yes, you are lucky, you know. You damned Anarchist, you've got Anarchist's luck, you have."

"Why's that," I said — it was in the summer of '19 and the Whites were chasing us hotfoot at the time, and darn' near catching us.

"I don't feel so lucky," I said. "Wait till we get out of this mess before you say I'm lucky."

"You don't know anything," said Alexei. "What I'm telling you is that you're lucky not to be in Moscow. They're shooting all the Anarchists in Moscow, and serve them right, the dirty dogs. They ought to shoot the whole lot of them, and serve them right."

It seems that there had been some trouble with the Anarchists in Moscow, and the Anarchists got sore. They made them a great big bomb, as big as a tar-barrel, so big that one man couldn't lift it, and they had to have two of them to carry it on a pole, like a tar-barrel. They took it to the garden of a house in the middle of Moscow where the Bolsheviks were holding a party meeting, not the biggest Bolsheviks but some pretty big ones. It was the middle of summer, and hot, and the meeting was on the first floor and the windows were open, wide open, to let in the mosquitoes, and maybe some cool air, or to let out the hot air the Bolsheviks were talking.

The two Anarchists took their bomb on its pole, hanging like a tar-barrel, and climbed up the wall of the garden overlooking the window of the room where the Bolsheviks were talking. You know how these Russians talk; they'd talk the hind leg off a goat, and when they talk they get excited and don't notice anything. They never thought of looking out the window, just talked and talked, and none of them looked out of the window. So the Anarchists swung the bomb; they swung it once, they swung it twice, and let it

137

go, right in through the open window. And it burst. Oh, yes, it burst all right; it broke windows in the Kremlin half a mile away. I tell you, that was a fine big burst those boys made to show the Bolsheviks what the Anarchists thought of them. It blew that Bolshevik meeting plumb to hell, you bet it did. And would you believe it, one of those bright Anarchists stood on the wall to see what happened. He did indeed, but he never *knew*, unless he compared notes with the Bolsheviks afterward, down in hell, because it blew him further than them and in smaller pieces. The other boy ducked behind a wall and only hurt his leg. He got away in the scuffle, got clear away, and didn't come back. Because Moscow wasn't healthy for Anarchists. Not after that it wasn't, you bet it wasn't. They shot five hundred that night and early the next morning.

So Alexei said to me, "You're lucky that you ain't in Moscow right now because they're swatting Anarchists like flies."

I said, "Hell, don't be silly. You'd get me out of it, wouldn't you? You're a Bolshevik and I'm a friend of yours. You'd save me, wouldn't you?"

That made him serious, and he said, "Sure, I would; you know that, Ed. From anyone, against anything, always; you know that." And he meant it, I knew he meant it. Ain't a guy lucky to have a friend like that, a real friend, if you know what I mean, like Alexei was to me.

What's love anyway? Just sex driving you to keep on going and keep the race going. They say love's stronger than death, they say it, but what do they *know*? I say the danger of death when you share it with a friend is stronger than love *and* sex. There are always girls, and some are better than others and some are worse, but always girls. Not always the same girls, but always the same. All the girls are the same always. I know that now, and I ought to of known it then, but I didn't, and that was the trouble. I mean that you never think of things until it's too late. Because girls don't like men to be real friends, not *their* men, they don't, not friends with another man.

138

I don't know why, but they don't like it. Or maybe I'm just a damned fool anyway, and *that* is the trouble. I've thought and I've thought and I can't find the answer; I know why *she* did it, but what should I have done.

You see, in the winter of '25, they sent me down on a trip through the Pamir Mountains. It was a hell of a trip with bandits after us like fleas and as dangerous and cold as the night wind in the mountains, right up there on the Roof of the World, as they call it. The night wind cut like a knife, and there was no shelter from it. You wanted to die rather than face it. I was lucky again to get out of that, with no worse than a frost-bitten finger.

When I got back to Moscow I saw one of the Big Boys, and he said we'd done fine, and: "Thank you, Comrade, this means the Order of Lenin for you. You've done well," he said, "and you've earned it." And I got it and I'd earned it. You bet we'd earned it, all of us on *that* expedition.

But there was a little fat ape of a bureaucrat who asked for my expense account. Just think of it! "We want vouchers," he said. "We want to know every kopeck that you spent on your trip, and where and why, with receipts for same. Yes," he said, "this country's run on a business basis nowadays. Maybe you soldiers don't know that yet, but I'm telling you," he said. "We want to know just what you spent and where and why, with vouchers."

"Where do you think I come from," I told him, "the State Bank or the mountains of Asia? You can chase yourself and your vouchers from the State Bank here in Moscow straight down to the Afghan border and the mountains of Pamir."

I walked out on him with three thousand rubles in my pocket. I'd of given it to him if he'd asked for it right; it was all I had left. Did he think I was trying to steal it? Steal it from whom, I'd like to know, from the bandits or the mountains or the snow blizzard.

So I walked out with the dough in my pocket, back to Alexei's apartment; of course I was staying with him. He had two rooms and

139

a Georgian girl with red lips and hot eyes and hair so slick and black it looked blue in the light, damn her soul.

Alexei was out when I got back from talking with the bureaucrat, and I had dinner with this girl of his, Tamara. We had some drinks and then we sat on the sofa, and maybe I did put my arm around her. What's the harm in that — I was just kidding, and . . . you know how it is. Then she looked at me sideways, the way they do, some of them, and said, "Eddaboy." (She always called me that because Alexei used to say 'Attaboy, Ed' — he'd caught that much American, but she got it muddled.) "Eddaboy," she said, looking sideways, "Alexei won't be home till midnight," and she squeezed closer under my arm.

I changed the subject quick and told her all about the bureaucrat and his vouchers and what I said to him and the money in my pocket all the time. I made it all gay and exciting, and jumped up to show how I spoke to him, and sat down again in Alexei's chair at his desk to show how the bureaucrat looked. I thought that was rather smart of me, to get away from the girl on the sofa. To make it a better story I said I was in danger. "He looked a tough little bird," I said, "and I made him sore. They don't like thieves in the Red Army," I told her, "not when they catch them. They shoot thieves in the Red Army, when they catch them." And that's not joking either, and it made me shiver just to think of it.

She sat there all thrilled with her eyes like hot coals. So I played up some more and said, "Yes, but they can't catch me. Maybe they will arrest me, but they can't catch me because I'm not a thief. I've got the money — look, it's all here in my wallet. I'll show these Moscow bureaucrats."

I thought I was being mighty smart, and just then there was a knock at the door and a bunch of Alexei's friends came in, but everything was nice and proper, just me and Tamara talking together across the room. Then we had a party, a wildish party, but nice and proper.

140

Lucky in Love

The last time I danced with Tamara I nearly slipped. Damn it, I'm human, ain't I; and she was a crazy one. I guess she thought she'd got me. She said, "Come on; they're all drunk, and who cares? Alexei won't be back for hours. Come on," she said, "they won't notice and who cares?"

But me and Alexei were friends, and she was his girl. So I told her, "Damn you, shut up. You can't get away with it," I said, "not with me you can't, not if you were the last girl on earth."

She went all limp, then snuggled up close again, right close with her arms on my neck, and whispered so faint I could hardly hear her, "I'm sorry, Eddaboy, so sorry. Isn't Alexei lucky to have a friend like you?"

The Young Luckinvar Anarchist stopped suddenly, and took a quick drink of vodka. He gulped over it twice, and there were tears in his eyes. But it was strong vodka, as I knew to my cost. Then he went on in a different voice, slow and not so loud.

"I don't know when Alexei came in, 'cause I went to sleep on the sofa, dead to the world. But the next morning, before nine it must have been, they waked me up all right, two guards, if you please, with bayonets, and a snappy young squirt of an officer dressed neat as a pin. They'd come to arrest me, account of that darned money. They told me to come along quick and make no fuss about it. Wouldn't even let me take a drink. I'd a hangover and a half, you understand, and my head ached like hell, but somehow I thought it would be fun to fool them, so I didn't say a word, just followed like a lamb. You see, I knew I had the money all the time, right there in my wallet, I'd never touched a cent of it.

"There was a hack at the door and they drove me somewhere — my head was aching so I took no notice — and ran me upstairs to an office where a big tough guy in uniform was sitting at a desk. Looked more like an American police captain, one of those hard-faced mugs, than a decent Russian.

141

"'Now, then, you,' he barked, 'what the hell have you been doing, and what's all this about money? Do you think we've got time to waste on a lot of thieving soldiers?'

"That made me sore, and I came right back at him. 'Thievin', nothin',' I said. 'I ain't stolen your money. But it turns me sick to have a little ape of a bureaucrat ask for vouchers, from the Pamirs, mind you! Or did he think I'd been making a trip to Leningrad? But I've got the money right here, three thousand rubles.'

"He looked kinda different at that, and said more friendly, 'Well, if that's so, there's nothing to worry about. Just hand it over and we'll fix the details later.'

"'Sure thing,' I said, and put my hand in my pocket. Was that a shock? It nearly knocked me dead. There was no wallet in the pocket, nor in any other pocket. I gaped at him with my mouth open like a fish.

"'Oh, yeah?' he said in a nasty voice. 'I suppose you've lost it somewhere, that's what they mostly say. Never mind, I'll deal with you later. I'm busy now.'

"I tried to explain, but he wouldn't listen. 'Shut up. You can tell me that later. I'm busy now,' and made a sign to the guards.

"Just at that moment in rushed Alexei, half-dressed, with his hair on end, and my wallet in his hand. He pulled up and saluted the captain. 'This man's story is true,' he said, without looking at me. 'I know all about it. He stayed with me, and I heard the noise when they came to arrest him. The money is here all right, I found it where — where he had left it.'

"The big guy took the money and counted it. 'Three thousand rubles, you said. That's right. Very well, you can go, but don't be such a fool again. Things happen to thieves in this country whether they wear uniform or not.'

"Out in the passage I turned to hug Alexei. 'My God,' I cried, 'you've done it again. Came right in the nick o'time. But — where on earth did you . . .'

142

"He shook me off like poison ivy.

"'Don't touch me. You know damn' well where I found it — under my own pillow — where you left it when you had your fun.' He raised his fist to hit me, then turned and bolted down the passage."

Again the young Anarchist stopped and took a drink, but this time there was no doubt; there were tears in his eyes before he swallowed the vodka.

Shatoff chuckled. "The little devil — I suppose she slipped it from your pocket at the end there when you wouldn't go with her, and put it under your buddy's pillow. You can't beat the little darlings, bless their souls."

Poor Luckinvar nodded without a word.

The Parrot

THE BOX-CAR rattled and swayed as the train jerked slowly out of the station, but the big sergeant standing at the open door balanced himself easily in his thick felt boots.

He held Sergey McTavish by the collar of his astrakhan tunic and the seat of his breeches, kicking and wriggling like a retriever pup. Then he swung the boy up level with his shoulder and threw him sprawling on a snowdrift.

"There," he said, "you young devil, that will teach you to steal potatoes from the army and sell them to dirty food speculators. You have the red head of an imp from hell, and the black heart of a capitalist. We have done with you."

So ended the six-months career of Sergey McTavish as mascot of the seventh battalion of Red Army Riflemen.

During those months he had tasted victory — in the swift advance to the gates of Warsaw — and defeat — in the hungry flight back across the frontier; he had come to swear like a Russian soldier, who swears with strength and zest; and he had looted gloriously — the astrakhan cloak on which the battalion tailor had worked all night, jolting cross-legged in a mule-cart, to make round cap, tunic and breeches. But he had not learned discipline or honesty; neither overcurrent in the Red Army of those days; and so here he was, gasping for breath on a snowdrift in the outskirts of a little town in the Ural foothills, while his late comrades jogged heedlessly on to their garrison at Ekaterinburg.

When he got his breath back, Sergey scrambled to his feet and turned to curse the big sergeant as worst he knew how. But the tail

144

of the train was blank and black in the December twilight, growing smaller every second, too small to be worth cursing. In the jargon of the Red Army, the episode was "liquidated".

Sergey Sergeyitch McTavish, twelve-year-old orphan, son of a Scottish soldier of fortune and a German farmer's daughter from the old Volga "colonies", was alone, friendless, penniless and hungry in a wind-swept freight-yard, with nothing in sight but the meager huts of the station and rows of roofless cars whose broken sides stuck out like jagged teeth. Sergey regretted now that he had been so smart and witty a few hours before at the expense of the station commandant, a thick-headed Lett. His comrades on the train had roared with laughter and kept off the angry Lett when Sergey dived among them for refuge. The light in the station hut meant warmth and food now, but Letts are a stubborn and unforgiving people. No, there was nothing for it but to tramp the three miles back to that dismal town.

Damn potatoes anyway, and speculators! If they had only left him the money! That brute of a sergeant had grabbed every kopeck. Still, he was lucky, at that; they might have beaten him or marooned him naked on the open steppe.

But a veteran of the Polish war knows worse things than hunger or cold or darkness. The boy dragged his cap down over his ears and set off across the rusty tracks toward the town.

As he crept under the second of three lines of dismantled freight-cars, his nose caught full blast the smell of cooking food. Right before him in the third row, one car was intact, light shining behind the little window in the door, and smoke pouring from the stovepipe at the roof-corner.

Without hesitation Sergey banged his fist upon the door. It slid open immediately, and a girl looked down at him.

"Come in, stranger," she cried. "We are expecting you. But tell me quickly is it to heaven or to hell that we owe the pleasure of your visit?"

The Parrot

"He who sent me here said I had the red head of an imp from hell," replied Sergey, swinging up by her outstretched hand and slamming the door behind him. "So you can understand I find it cold here, and am hungry, after my journey."

The girl brushed off his cap and pulled him forward under the kerosene lamp which hung from the middle of the roof.

"Red as hell's flames," she muttered admiringly. "That should keep you warm, and we will fill your belly. My father, here, just said it would take a saint or a devil to conquer my problem, and I told him as you knocked, that even Saint Nicholas the Wonder-worker would never dare risk his wings in Russia today."

A roar of laughter from a heap of straw in the corner near the stove. "'Tis but a little imp for so great a task, Marfoosha, and I doubt if the Prince of Devils himself is a match for the Baba Papa-gai, who beyond doubt is his own grandmother." The voice shook a trifle over the last words, and Sergey glimpsed fingers gesturing quickly over a broad khaki chest.

There were three people in the car, the girl, comely and slim with a tangle of blonde hair, red shirt tucked into short blue kilt and high black leather boots; the man, in khaki uniform, lying on the straw, fat brown cheeks, quick little black eyes in a bush of iron-gray hair and whiskers; and a small bent figure by the stove, so wrapped in a service overcoat of the old Imperial army that nothing was visible but a white wisp of beard, a bald shining pate and two pink pointed ears.

"Comrade imp," said the girl, "I present my grandfather, who lives alone in this car, being wise and having money, but not wise enough to help me in my trouble; and my father, who is commandant of the prison, but unable to save my lover, his prisoner, from . . ."

"Don't forget to present Comrade Soup also," broke in the old man with a chuckle, "and little Comrade Vodka in his bottle, who is best of all." And, plunging an iron ladle into the steaming pot, he filled an earthen bowl and passed it to the hungry boy.

146

The Parrot

Twice Sergey emptied the bowl, breaking chunks of black bread into the hot liquid. Then he gulped a stinging mouthful of spirit from the bottle, and taking a palmful of green flake "*mahorka*," and a scrap of newspaper from the old man, twisted the cone-shaped cigarette of the Russian soldier, lighted the upturned flap with a sulphur match and putting the small end of the cone between his lips, puffed out a cloud of evil-smelling smoke.

"What is this trouble you speak of," he asked, "and who is the Parrot Woman, the Baba Papagai?"

All three of his hosts spoke at once, in noisy excitement. There was a young man, a foreigner, a prisoner, an American, a soldier, who had come somehow from somewhere eastward on a train, young and cheerful and clever with his hands beyond belief; and the girl Marfoosha loved him, and he had mended the electric light for the prison and later for the whole town, and at first he was quite dumb like a beast, but now he spoke humanly enough after several months; and two weeks ago the Soviet had agreed to let Marfoosha marry him, because they wanted to keep him in the town to start again the nail factory as he had promised, and because he was cheerful and had blue eyes and brown curly hair, and Marfoosha loved him and wanted to marry him terribly, and would die too if he were killed.

This Sergey learned first, because the girl talked fastest and loudest, but through it all beat like the drum in a regimental band the name of the Parrot Woman, Baba Papagai, who was a witch and a demon and the grandmother of all the devils. Bit by bit the boy got clear about her also and linked her up with Marfoosha and the American prisoner.

She had a familiar spirit, this terrible woman, a parrot, red and gray, in a wire cage; and when it bit you, you were guilty; and when it didn't, you were innocent; but it always bit you, and so you were always shot.

147

The Parrot

Nobody knew where she came from, but it was said she was the widow of a famous revolutionary who had worked in a factory at Ekaterinburg, and had been shot by the Czar's army in 1906. And now she was president of a "Flying Tribunal," that moved about the whole province judging counter-revolutionaries; and always she made them put a finger in the parrot's cage, and always it bit them, and then they were shot. And it was reported that she lived on the smell of blood and must kill a man every day or she would die and the Devil, her grandson, would fly off with her. And when the Soviet knew she was coming to hold court in the town, they were all very frightened, because there was only one victim, the ex-manager of the factory, who twice had tried to escape from the town and had been prevented. One man would never be enough for the Baba Papagai. She would suspect the Soviet of being lukewarm in the cause of revolution, and perhaps put some of them to the trial of that horrid parrot, as had happened before elsewhere, always with fatal results.

So four days ago the Soviet had held a meeting hastily and in secret, and had decided to sacrifice their American. They were sorry, but it was his head or theirs, no argument was possible. They'd put high hopes on his re-opening the factory; but after all, he was a stranger and a prisoner, and it was said the Americans were fighting to help the counter-revolution, and it was he or they, and finally there was just a chance that the parrot wouldn't like the taste of foreigners and fail to bite him.

Marfoosha and her father, who, as prison-commandant, felt most uneasy about the whole affair, had come to ask the advice of the hermit in the boxcar. But he had been of no help to them, and the father had said it would take an angel or a devil to find the way out of the mess, and just at that second Sergey had knocked, and said at once he was an imp from hell, so what would he suggest?

Sergey's Scotch blood whispered caution. He puffed his *mahorka*

148

cigarette and declared profoundly that there was a solution for every problem, but this case being extremely difficult, he had better set eyes first on the woman and her parrot, to say nothing of the American and the ex-manager of the factory, before deciding what should be done. There was a twinkle in Marfoosha's eye as she received his verdict, and the boy was reassured as to the reality of her belief in his diabolic origin; but the prison commandant and his elderly parent were ready in approval.

"Never drive pigs too swiftly," said the ancient, banging the cork of his vodka-bottle hard against the side of the car, and burying it in the recesses of his great coat. "Let our Comrade Imp view the situation for himself, and maybe he will be able to make a plan. For me, I am at a loss — I admit it freely; the young man must die: there is no doubt of it."

"Everyone must die some day," replied his son, "and I, as commandant of a prison, know that some die quicker than others. But this American is a friendly youth, and clever with his hands, and Marfoosha loves him dearly; so I want his life saved and no trouble with this infernal old woman. If the flame-headed Imp can help us, I, Alexei Petrovich, promise that he shall have all the food he needs in this cold country, and a warm corner by my fire to toast his toes till they are red as his hair."

All of which sounded good to Sergey McTavish as he said good-by to the old man, and accompanied Marfoosha and her father across the cold white plain to the little town.

Far off, beneath the low roofs of the town, windows poured a flood of light upon the snow.

"What makes your town so bright?" asked Sergey, tramping a little ahead of Marfoosha, step for step with the long strides of her father.

"I told you the American fixed our electric machines for us," said the prison warden. "I guess you are surprised to see one of our towns using electricity these days."

149

The Parrot

He emphasized the word "our" with a faintly sneering accent. It is a habit the Russians have, to deprecate everything Russian.

"And now," he went on mournfully, "even this town won't have any electricity any more. When he's gone, the whole works will be *kaput* in no time. Oh, that Baba Papagai and her parrot! To think that a miserable bird could bring such trouble upon us!"

"You say it's a bird?" asked Sergey, who had never seen a parrot in his life and had not the least idea whether it was bird or beast or perhaps a new kind of Soviet commissar. "Well, if it's only a bird that's worrying you, why don't you kill it?"

"Kill it!" almost shouted Marfoosha. "Why, you might as well talk of killing Lenin!"

"Shh!" cried her father sharply. "You mustn't talk like that!" He caught Sergey by the shoulder. "See here, little comrade, you don't understand. It's not a bird, really; it only looks like a bird. But it talks like a man, and it tells her, the Baba, what she must do. Who shall say which is the master, the parrot or the parrot woman? Everyone knows there are things like that, which come out of the dark to serve those who sell their souls to Darkness. You can't kill them, ever, the dark spirits, but in the old days a priest could drive them away with the name of God and holy water. And now the priests are spat upon and hide in holes, and God has turned His face from our Russia, which is become a plaything for the evil ones." His voice sank into a whimper and he crossed himself with bowed head. The girl stood motionless, but her breath came in short gasps as if she had been running.

Sergey McTavish shivered. This was ill talk, of spirits from the dark, and the man's fear was infectious. But he bit tight on the life-rule which had steeled him and his father and his father's father who died to check Osman Pasha's last sortie from Plevna — "No Scot can show fear before a Russian."

"That is stuff for women and children," he said stoutly: "but we

150

men of the Red Army care neither for gods nor devils; and besides, why worry about the ford till you come to the river?"

His companions made no answer, and all three trudged on in silence through the snow.

The prison was a large house set back among tall trees whose branches hung glittering with frost in the light of an electric arc-lamp. A sentry bundled to the ears in bearskin coat peered at them through the rime of his collar, then stood aside with a thump of his bayoneted gun upon the doorstep.

In the high, square entrance hall two men were sitting before a huge fireplace, ablaze with round birch logs thick as a man's body. The younger leaped up as they entered, tall and loose-limbed, in a uniform of dark mustard color such as Sergey had never seen. In two strides, so it seemed, he was across the room, lifting Marfoosha right off her feet into his arms.

There was more delight than anger in her squeal of protest. Sergey stood watching, round-eyed, while the girl's father walked forward to join the other men beside the fire.

"Enough, Mahlinkie, enough," cried Marfoosha in a stifled voice. "Put me down — we have a visitor, bad-mannered one!"

Regaining her feet, she flung her arm round Sergey's shoulder. "This is my American, little comrade; his name is Djim, but that is a dog's name, not a man's, so I call him Mahlinkie, the little one, because he is so tall." She laughed gayly and pushed the boy forward, pulling off his hat with her other hand. "Look, Mahlinkie, it's fire, but it doesn't burn." And she ran her fingers through Sergey's flaming hair.

"Fortheluvamike!"

Sergey McTavish did not understand this American greeting, but something within him called forth two half-forgotten words in reply. "Scottish, gorrd-am-you-sirr."

The Parrot

The effect was startling. High in the air went Sergey in those strong young arms, while a torrent of unfamiliar words beat upon his ears. What a din they made! Sergey, six feet from the ground, beside himself with excitement, yelling his newfound slogan; the American shouting strange noises, and Marfoosha dancing around them, half in laughter, half in tears.

The prison warden and his friend by the fire rushed forward in panic. "Are you mad?" cried the former, catching his daughter around the waist. "Stop this uproar. You don't know what's happened. She is here already, staying in Petrusha's house."

Marfoosha halted as if struck by lightning, and the American stiffened, holding Sergey in mid-air.

Slowly he lowered the boy to the ground, still grasping him firmly under the arms. An instant's silence; then the warden continued: "She came tonight, with her parrot — saints defend us — and holds court tomorrow. Very angry when she heard there were only two cases. She will judge the factory manager in the morning; and the next day" — he jerked his thumb towards the American — "it's his turn. They say we are lucky. He's a foreigner — she was quite interested and said no more about our scarcity of prisoners."

There was no answer to these words save a low sound from Marfoosha. She had fainted.

Sergey McTavish awoke next morning from a tormenting dream of gray devil-birds with red tails pecking at his breast, to find Marfoosha and her American standing beside the bench on which he had passed the night before the fire.

The girl's face was red and swollen with weeping, but her lover wore a friendly grin.

"Wake up, little comrade, wake up and eat your breakfast, for there's work for you to do." She had tried to speak cheerfully, but as Sergey rubbed his eyes she sank down in a heap beside the bench, sobbing desperately.

152

The Parrot

The tall American tried vainly to comfort her: "Marfoosha, my darling, my baby girl, don't worry."

Sergey McTavish sat upright. How stupid girls were, not to understand that death was part of a soldier's job! He pulled Marfoosha's hair sharply. "Stop crying," he said, "and tell me what's the matter."

Marfoosha shook herself free. "All right," she said to her lover, "but you go and let me talk to him alone."

And then to Sergey: "The Baba Papagai is in a frightful humor. We know it from Petrusha. She had her parrot at breakfast with her, early, two hours ago before it was light, and sat there talking, talking. She said to him, '*Belogvardeyetz*' (White Guard), and the parrot answered '*Belogvardeyetz*', and then the Baba Papagai laughed and the parrot said over and over again, '*Belogvardeyetz*,' and the Baba Papagai laughed some more.

"You, Sergey Sergeyitch, do you know what that means?" Marfoosha leaned across the bench and laid her clenched fists close to Sergey's heart.

"No," said Sergey uneasily, with a spoonful of *kasha* poised halfway to his lips.

"Death! That's all! Just death for my American!" Marfoosha laid her head on her arms, then straightened up and rattled on breathlessly:

"The court opens at ten o'clock. You go there. It will be just a general rehearsal. The Baba Papagai is having her rehearsal this morning. The real show is when my American comes before her." Marfoosha's voice faltered. Sergey again stopped eating.

"She knows it. She told Petrusha she had heard of this American in town. She said she had never before had the chance to try her *papagai* on an American. She cursed America. She said it was the sink of all iniquity, a den of wolves, the castle of capitalism. She said that all Americans were White Guards, and when she said

153

The Parrot

'American' to her parrot this morning, it just answered '*Belog-vardeyetz.*'

"Sergey, go see for yourself."

Sergey put the half-empty *kasha* bowl on the floor. He had lost his appetite. It was clear to him that Marfoosha was all wrought up about this business, but, hoping against despair, somehow looked to him to help her.

"What time is it?" he asked.

"Near ten," answered Marfoosha. "Come with me — I'll show you the way." Outside, the sun was rising red through the mist over the blank white steppe.

Ten minutes from her home Marfoosha stopped, took Sergey by the arm and pointed straight ahead.

"There it is," she said.

"What, the church?" asked Sergey.

"It used to be the church. Don't you see the guard in front? Now go, please, and come to us as soon as it is over." Marfoosha took Sergey's head in her arms, pressed it to her heart until he struggled to get free, then released him with a push and, turning swiftly, ran back the way they had come.

Sergey McTavish recovered his balance, frowned a moment at the retreating figure, then proceeded warily toward the church. There was nothing strange to him about a Cheka trial taking place there. Even when other buildings were available, the "Flying Tribunals of the All Russian Extraordinary Commission for Combating Counter-Revolutions" had found that their sessions made a far greater impression on their White Guard enemies if they were held in the church. It appealed, too, to the Red sense of humor.

In front of the building, beneath an ikon of the Virgin Mary, a Red Guard paced up and down, his conical cap pulled tight over his ears to meet the threadbare collar of an old gray overcoat. The buttons, cut off because they had borne the insignia of the Czar, were replaced with string. When Sergey approached, the Red Guard dropped the butt of his rifle nonchalantly in the snow, crying, "What do you want, little princeling?" with an ironic wink at the boy's astrakhan suit.

"Don't call me names, comrade," grinned back Sergey. "I'm Red Army too. This is loot from the Polaks, issued me by the regimental tailor, Seventh Battalion Rifles. Just lost touch with headquarters. Now be a good comrade and give me a cigarette and let me go inside and get warm a bit."

The sentry laughed, said he'd no tobacco but obligingly turned his back while Sergey slipped past into the church.

For a moment he could see nothing in the dim interior save two tall candles on the altar above which an ikon glittered with gold and jewels.

Very quietly he groped his way forward to the last of a number of rough wooden benches which had been placed in the nave, and sat down behind rows of people bent forward in eager attention. At the other end of the church a man was speaking in a high-pitched voice, trailing off at times into falsetto. The words came rapidly, tumbling over one another, hardly intelligible. Sergey could only catch a phrase now and then — "never. . . . Czar's government . . . always tried to work for the people . . . worker myself . . . not my fault . . . education . . . no counter-revolutionary, believe me, believe me, believe me."

Cutting this babble like a saw, another voice, metallic, harsh, rasped a single word: "*Belogvardeyetz!*" (White Guard)

Then a loud laugh. Then silence.

Sergey's eyes, by now accustomed to the semi-darkness, sought the source of the inhuman voice. With a shiver of interest he realized the word "*Belogvardeyetz!*" had come from a cage swinging beneath a stiff gold embroidery attached like a banner to a pole, which stood at the left of the altar. Within the cage a gray-red bird moved

The Parrot

listlessly on its perch. That was the bird that talked like a man, but who had laughed?

Near the altar a woman was rising to her feet behind a table draped with red cloth. Erect, she loomed enormous, six feet or more in height. Traces of mocking laughter were still about her lips, but her eyes bore no sign of it. The flickering light gleamed on abnormally protruding eyeballs, threw into relief a network of swollen veins on either temple, and showed her thickened throat bursting from the collar of a soldier's tunic.

Sergey felt his hands shake as they fumbled for his pockets. He needed no one to tell him this was the Baba Papagai.

With a gesture of impatience she pulled off the cap, revealing a thin growth of gray hair. The woman was nearly bald.

She turned to the left where a man was standing, thin and crumpled, between two soldiers with fixed bayonets.

"Counter-revolutionary!" she bellowed suddenly. The man staggered. He moistened his lips with the end of his tongue and seemed to be trying to speak, but before the words came, the Baba Papagai continued more quietly:

"I know what you want to say, citizen. You never carried on counter-revolution. You never harmed or oppressed anyone, never resisted the proletariat; in fact, you admire the revolution intensely and think Lenin and Trotsky the greatest men in history. Yes, I know all that; I've heard the same story before, often." Her voice deepened and again became harsh. She wiped her mouth with the back of her hand and resumed: "Fortunately, fortunately, we have here with us the means of seeing beneath those fine words, right to the inner secrets of your heart. You are surprised, perhaps, that an ignorant old woman like me should see, should be able to know the secret heart of an 'intelligenter' like you; but I don't pretend so much. It is this wise bird here, who is older than I, older, it may be, than anyone in this town, who by long experience can recognize a

156

counter-revolutionary at first glance, can smell the black soul of him in one sniff."

Her voice had become monotonous, rising and falling like that of a priest reciting some familiar ritual.

"Walk forward, my friend of the people, walk forward, and put your finger into the cage of my little comrade, that he may take a sniff at it. Perhaps you are innocent, as you would have us believe. The little comrade will know, because he never makes a mistake. If you are innocent, he will do you no harm, will not touch your finger; but if your hand has offended against the People," — again that inhuman roar, — "he will bite it to the bone, and after my judgment, you shall receive your punishment."

She made a sign to the soldiers, who took the cringing man by the arms and dragged him toward the parrot's cage. The man shrank within his coat as if wishing to wither up and slip out of his clothes, leaving them in the hands of his guards. They grasped him more firmly and urged him forward. The candle-light glanced from their bayonets and played across the bulging eyes of the Baba Papagai as she mockingly reassured the terror-stricken figure in their hands.

"Have no fear, little servant of dogs. That bird is a proletarian. You said you loved the workers. If it's true, the *papagai* will never touch you. Nor will I."

There was no sound save the prisoner's feet dragging across the floor as the soldiers carried him to the last instance of justice. He had slumped down in their arms so that when they reached the foot of the golden banner, his head fell in the shadow cast by the bottom of the cage. In the attempt to raise him upright, the guards brought his forehead heavily against it. The impact shook the parrot. It ruffled its feathers, stretched its wings, brought them tightly back against its body and hopped expectantly forward on its perch. Its indifference was gone; its beady eyes were watchful.

157

The Parrot

A murmur of awe, or wonderment, or horror, floated from the shadowy figures which filled the benches. It was cut short by the voice of the Baba Papagai.

"Carry out the procedure, Soldiers of the Revolution. If the servant of dogs cannot lift his hand, lift it for him."

The prisoner struggled. One of the soldiers deftly twisted the left arm of the writhing man behind his back and pushed it upward until he gasped: "I'll do it." The soldier released the pressure on the twisted arm and the prisoner stood upright. He lifted his right hand with extended forefinger and thrust it forward by short jerks. Twice he dropped his hand, and twice the soldier pressed the hammer-lock until he gasped again: "I'll do it."

The third time, his finger reached the cage. It trembled so that he was unable to poke it through the bars. The other guard grasped it firmly and pushed it into the cage. For a moment there was utter stillness in the church. The prisoner had raised his head and was staring with fascinated eyes at the parrot. He watched the bird as though the finger in the cage was another man's.

The parrot eyed the prisoner's hand. Cocking its head on one side, it cast its beady gaze appraisingly at the forefinger that shook as though playfully just below its beak. Its claws against the perch made a faint scratching sound which seemed to reverberate in the silence. A peasant seated on the front bench crossed himself mechanically.

The parrot bent its neck, and — rubbed its beak on the perch. Sergey almost laughed. Then he caught the first expulsion of breath, half choked and gasped, as he saw the parrot lunge forward swiftly, take the finger with a snapping motion in its beak and bite downward.

More shocking than any scream was the silence of the prisoner. The parrot had bitten him to the bone. He behaved as though he had not felt it. Such a relief, this stab of pain, from the slow torture of suspense, so welcome the knowledge of his doom after its uncer-

158

tainty, that the bird's bite, though meaning death, was like a douche of cold water, reviving his manhood.

"*Belogvardeyetz!*" croaked the parrot, back on its perch with one strong wingbeat.

"He never makes a mistake," exclaimed the Baba Papagai, and gabbled formally: "Citizen Nikitin, this court finds you guilty of counter-revolution.

"Take him out!" she shouted. "To the cellar with the White Guard servant of dogs!"

The prisoner was the calmest man in the church. Erect, his head back, with a firm step he allowed his guards to lead him across the front of the altar toward the rear entrance. As he passed the table of the Baba Papagai, she leaned forward and feasted her bulging eyes on his drawn white face. The prisoner looked her back squarely, sneering as though in sympathy with the snarl on her face, and with a contemptuous cry, "Parrot justice!" yielded to the urging of his guards as they dragged him through the door.

The Baba Papagai put on the cloth cap. Her upper lip clamped down in savage determination. "Tonight, at eleven o'clock, we'll hear the next case on the docket." She gathered up her papers, shoved the table aside, and strode down the aisle.

Court was adjourned.

Sergey had intended to slip out before the others, but he had not reckoned with this abrupt ending of the session. Before he could move, the Baba Papagai was in the aisle, scrutinizing the faces as she passed. With every step she took, his courage waned. By the time she reached his bench, he was huddled cowering in his seat. He felt numb in the clutch of a nightmare. Those eyes were the eyes of a Kelpie, that monster from the stories of Scotland his father had told him long ago, half-bull, half-demon, but shaped like a man, which dwelt at the bottom of the deep lochs of the Highlands and on nights when the full moon shone, appeared beside the skiffs of unwary boatmen and dragged them down to death. The Kelpie, he recollected shudderingly, had just such bulging eyes, such shaggy eyebrows, such lineaments of hate.

Never before had Sergey known such anguish as when the Baba Papagai stopped beside him, turned and surveyed the church to satisfy herself no one had moved since she left her table, then, quite accidentally let fall her gaze on his small red head.

The Baba Papagai apparently felt the need to emphasize her exit.

"Well, who are you, with your head of an imp from hell?" boomed the cruel voice.

This repetition of the phrase so fresh in his memory broke the spell sufficiently for him to stammer out: "I'm only a little boy."

"Whelp!" spat the Baba Papagai, and passed on through the door.

Sergey waited motionless until nearly everyone had left the building.

Running back to the prison as fast as he could, Sergey felt the movement of his legs in the sharp air send the blood tingling through his veins, and by the time he reached the house and paused to scrape the snow from his boots, he had shaken off his fears. He felt big with importance as he entered the hall and knew that he had news to tell. Marfoosha's face brought back the unaccustomed sense of depression. She was sitting at the table between her father and the American soldier, her head sunk on her breast.

The two men looked up eagerly when Sergey appeared, but Marfoosha never stirred.

"Well, what happened?" cried the commandant.

"It bit, all right," announced Sergey in a matter of fact tone.

The prison warden shoved his glass away from him, banged his fist on the table: "I knew it."

Marfoosha lifted her head as if just awakened. Catching Sergey by the arm she drew him to her and whispered: "Tell us about it. All about it."

160

Sergey began. They listened as though their lives depended upon every word.

"And then," he went on, "she said she would hold court again tonight."

"Tonight?" all three broke out. "Tonight? It was to be to-morrow."

"You mean," gasped Marfoosha, "that — that — he is to be tried tonight?"

"That's what she said," responded Sergey.

Marfoosha threw herself on the floor, clasping her lover round the knees. "They shan't. They shan't!" she screamed.

His face was white and his lip trembled a little as he patted her head, repeating tenderly: "*Nichevo, nichevo, nichevo.*" It was the only Russian word he could pronounce without a trace of accent, the universal "Never mind" or "What's the use," of Slavic fatalism.

But his caressing hand froze when the commandant mumbled thickly: "They shoot you through the back of the head."

Marfoosha sobbed aloud.

"Yes, that's how they do it," insisted her father, tipsy with indignation. "They take you down to the cellar of the church and just as you pass the threshold they shoot you in the back of the head. They think you wont expect it, and wont turn around, and that it's the easiest way to get it over. But lots do know. The dirty swine!"

A moan from his daughter checked him suddenly, diverting his anger: "And you! You damned imp!" he yelled at Sergey, "What are you going to do? I thought you could find something?"

Marfoosha's weary, "Let him alone," roused her father to a higher pitch.

"No, I wont let him alone. What good has he done? You damned imp! It was Dedushka who swore you amounted to something. The old man is getting crazier every day. Suppose you get along over there and let him know how worthless you are. Get on. Get out of

161

here." Unable to vent his feelings otherwise, the commandant staggered to his feet and advanced with threatening fist toward the boy.

Sergey retreated sullenly. He was halfway down the steps when the commandant rushed out and yelled at him: "What time will it be?"

"Eleven o'clock tonight," shouted the boy without pausing.

It was already past five o'clock and pitch dark. He found his way through the town by the glow from the windows and afterward by instinct, like a young wild animal, accurately retraced the path of the evening before. His thoughts were whirling about the awful eyes of the Baba Papagai. The longer he thought, the more convinced he became that she was a Kelpie. His father's stories came back more vividly. Surely there was some detail he had forgotten. Yes, something about a charm or talisman against the monster. His father certainly had spoken of a charm. But that was all so long ago. To Sergey a whole lifetime seemed to have passed since then, and he groped back in his memory as an old man strives to recall his youth. He tried to concentrate his mind on the talisman, but each time it slipped away from him. "Like a watermelon seed slipping through your fingers," thought Sergey.

The simile struck a vein of association. The talisman was some kind of seed. His boots brushed against the branches of a fir tree growing beside the railroad track. Sergey felt as though a door in his mind had opened halfway.

"Tree berries! The berries of the mountain ash! That's what Father said was good for Kelpies. Woven in a cross."

But something else too, when there were no ash berries. Something still better, he reflected. The feeling that the door was only halfway open persisted. He was walking head down, so absorbed in the effort to remember that he went past the old man's box-car without noticing it. Suddenly he stopped, sniffed the air like a

162

hound on the trail, turned, saw the box-car and ran toward it. He continued to sniff as he banged on the door, stamping impatiently until it opened with a puff of savory steam.

"I've found it!" shouted Sergey, leaping up and seizing the astonished old man by the hand. "I've found it!" he repeated, dancing in excitement. "We can save him now."

"In the name of the Holy Saints Boris and Gleb!" ejaculated the grandfather. "What is it you've found to make you jump like a flea on a frog's back?"

Sergey hardly heard him. His eyes were roving round the cabin. "Ha! There, in the corner!" He heaved a deep sigh of relief. "The charm!" he exclaimed. "The charm, little grandfather, the charm to defeat the Kelpie."

"And now perhaps you'll tell me what a Kelpie is, and why you're behaving like an idiot," grunted the old man sarcastically as he dipped a bowl of stew and placed it smoking hot before the boy. How good it smelled! Sergey recollected his stomach so keenly that he forgot his excitement. Over the stew he related the day's events, dwelling on his conviction that the Baba Papagai was a Kelpie.

"Very probable. Very probable." The old man nodded affirmatively and looked with as much wonder as old age can feel at the red head of his small visitor bobbing up and down over the bowl.

"Whew, I'm late, terribly late. Maybe he's already gone. Must run like the devil."

Sergey jumped for the door, pulling his fur cap over his ears, and with a shrill "Good-bye!" bolted into the night.

He took the steps at the prison door in one jump, landed on his heels, skidded and fell in a heap at the feet of the surprised sentry.

"Gangway!" he gasped. "Lemme in."

"Who, then, is holding you?" said the sentry as Sergey jerked open the door and rushed into the hall.

It was empty.

163

The Parrot

Sergey stopped, frozen with the fear that he had come too late to give his talisman to the American. His feet lagged as he crossed the hall, but voices in a room beyond quickened his step. He pushed his head cautiously through the door, entered quickly, closed it with a bang and jumped forward. Marfoosha and the American were sitting on the floor, talking so earnestly that they scarcely heeded Sergey's presence. On the bed lay the prison commandant, groaning and panting. He was drunk.

Sergey brought his two hands down thwack on the backs of Marfoosha and her lover.

"Come! Quick! I've found it — the charm — to save you. Where's the kitchen? Come with me." His words brought the two instantly to their feet, and the commandant rolled his eyes, trying to get up.

"Quick! Here!" Sergey grabbed the American with his right hand and was digging in his pocket with the other when the Red Guard brusquely shoved him aside with: "Out of the way now, and enough of this monkey business. Can't help it. Orders is orders. Come along."

Marfoosha threw her arms around her lover's neck. The Red Guard frowned with embarrassment but paused. Sergey turned his back as though in sympathy with the feelings of the lovers, but in the moment of their embrace he pulled from his pocket a little white object, and clenching it tightly in his fist whirled and cried:

"Well, comrade, shake hands. Come on, be a man — don't stand there like a dummy."

The American looked down at him, smiled, released Marfoosha and took Sergey's small paw.

"Good-bye," he said.

"A talisman. Keep it in your hand until the last minute," whispered Sergey. "It's magic. Hold it tight, dig you nails into it, and you can't lose." Then loud: "Good-bye, comrade."

164

The Parrot

The heavy door of the house clanged shut, but Marfoosha stood where they had left her. Then she sank to her knees.

"Holy Saint Martha, thou who hast suffered greatly —"

The Baba Papagai believed in ceremony of a kind.

As eleven boomed from the tower, the Baba Papagai's huge bulk moved down the aisle towards the altar. Behind her two soldiers, each carrying a lighted candle, a yard long and thick as a man's arm. Behind them a third, holding aloft the golden banner, with the parrot's cage, wrapped in a white napkin swinging beneath it like a censer. Then the clerk of the court with measured step. Then two guards with fixed bayonets. Then the prisoner, head high, shoulders squared, marching slow as a funeral parade. Finally, two more guards, stolid, ponderous.

The Baba Papagai strode to the table before the altar, turned, surveyed the audience, seated herself and folded her arms. The man with the ecclesiastical banner placed it neatly in its socket, and with a nervous gesture flicked off the cover from the cage. The light of the two candles fell on the parrot. It blinked, ruffled its feathers, stretched its neck and croaked: "*Gotova!*" (Ready).

The Baba Papagai bared her yellow fangs.

"*Gotova!* Yes, we are ready, my little dove!

"Comrades," said the Baba Papagai, pushing back her chair, crossing her legs and shoving her cap to the back of her head. "Comrades, we are here tonight to try a foreign dog who was sent to impose the might of his capitalist masters upon the workers and peasants of the Russian Socialist Federation of Soviet Republics. He comes from the country which above all would like to see the first Workers and Peasants Government once more enslaved by tyrants. An American! It means a dog."

The word "dog" aroused the parrot. It squawked: "*Belogvardeyetz!*"

165

The Parrot

The woman's maniac laughter shocked the echoes of the church.

"Never wrong! Never wrong! My little dove never mistakes them," she cried. "Now, you dog of a White Guard, speak now for yourself. Say why you, a foreigner, dared invade our country."

The American answered boldly in his childish Russian:

"*Yah gavaryou ochen malo po Russky. No yah ne vinovat.*"

"Oh, you speak very little Russian but you're not guilty. You know enough to say that. And you've nothing more to say?" The Baba Papagai rose to her feet, placed her cap before her on the table and leaned forward. "Nothing more? Or have you some excuse?"

"*Nichevo*," retorted the prisoner coolly. It was the one word he pronounced perfectly in Russian.

Her face darkened with fury.

"Dog!" The word hissed to the farthest corners of the building. Immediately the parrot responded: "*Belogvardeyetz!*"

"The little comrade has spoken. Let him judge the case."

The two guards beside the American grasped him by the arms. He needed no urging. "*Nichevo*," he said, again, to tell them he was not afraid to play his part without coercion.

He walked straight up to the cage. Sergey held his breath. The boy's glance shifted rapidly from the parrot's cage to the Baba Papagai, still leaning forward on the table, her Kelpie's eyes a-goggle at her victim.

"Hell!" said the American aloud. The foreign word rang out defiantly. "Hell!" he repeated again, and stuck his forefinger into the cage.

The parrot lifted its wings. Every spectator — save perhaps one, for Sergey's Scotch heart beat stoutly in his breast — knew that it would strike. It lifted its wings, squawked, teetered on its perch, lowered its beak close to the proffered finger, then half flew, half hopped across the cage, beating the air, screeching atrociously: "*Konchala! Konchala!*" ("Finished! Finished!")

166

"Well? What do you say to that, old girl?" asked the American in English, grinning at the Baba Papagai.

Her eyes were glazed. She crashed her fist upon the table.

"Dog! Dog!" she roared.

"*Belogvardeyetz! Belogvardeyetz!*" weakly echoed the parrot.

"Once more, you dog!" commanded the Baba Papagai.

"As often as you like," answered the American, and put his finger again through the bars.

This time the parrot never pretended to investigate. It cowered at the bottom of the cage, buried its beak in its breast feathers, and only when the Baba Papagai shrieked "Dog!" at the top of her voice did it respond with a low croak: "*Belogvardeyetz!*"

"What's the hour?" The Baba Papagai turned to the clerk beside her. Trembling, he pulled from beneath his sheepskin coat a massive gold repeater, said, "Fifteen minutes to midnight," and returned the former property of the Prince Rashkushin to his pocket.

"Release the prisoner. He is acquitted." The parrot woman kicked aside her table and strode down the aisle. For the sake of this one victim she could not disavow her favorite instrument of terror.

This time Sergey Sergeyitch McTavish sat up straight in his seat and stared at her as she passed him. The moment she disappeared, he ran forward and grasped the American by the hand.

"A Kelpie! I told you! A Kelpie!" he yelled crazily. "My father was right — my father knew."

Indifferent to the buzz of congratulations and the eager hands outstretched to them, the young soldier swung Sergey aloft.

"You're all right, kid," he shouted in English. "You may be cuckoo, but you're there with the goods." Then in Russian: "What was it, *malchik*? I kept it in my hand until the last, but afterward I dropped it. How did you do it?"

His mouth close to the other's ear, Sergey murmured: "Take a sniff at your finger."

167

The Parrot

The American gave a loud yell, then checked himself.

"Yes," whispered Sergey, "garlic — that's the charm against Kelpies."

The two set off at a trot for the home of Marfoosha.

168

www.ingramcontent.com/pod-product-compliance
Lightning Source LLC
Chambersburg PA
CBHW032014240626
47153CB00003B/1248